WINTER SEA

Also by Alan Ross

Poetry
POEMS 1942–67
THE TAJ EXPRESS
OPEN SEA
DEATH VALLEY
AFTER PUSAN

General
COLOURS OF WAR
THE TURF (EDITOR)
THE EMISSARY

Travel
TIME WAS AWAY
THE GULF OF PLEASURE
THE BANDIT ON THE BILLIARD TABLE

Autobiography
BLINDFOLD GAMES
COASTWISE LIGHTS

Cricket
AUSTRALIA 55
CAPE SUMMER
THROUGH THE CARIBBEAN
AUSTRALIA 63
WEST INDIES AT LORD'S
THE CRICKETER'S COMPANION (EDITOR)
RANJI

Alan Ross

WINTER SEA

War, Journeys, Writers

THE HARVILL PRESS
LONDON

PR
6035
.0673
Z476
1997

First published in 1997 by
The Harvill Press
84 Thornhill Road
London N1 1RD

1 3 5 7 9 8 6 4 2

Several of the poems in Part V first appeared in
the *London Review of Books* and *P. N. Review*.
The author wishes to thank the editors

The permission of Gyldendal Norsk Forlag
to quote from the poetry of Nordahl Grieg
is gratefully acknowledged

Alan Ross asserts the moral right to be
identified as the author of this work

A CIP catalogue record for this title is available
from the British Library

ISBN 1 86046 431 9

Designed and typeset in Baskerville at
Libanus Press, Marlborough, Wiltshire

Printed and bound in Great Britain by Butler & Tanner Ltd
at Selwood Printing, Burgess Hill

CONTENTS

PART I

Tallinn–Haapsalu

THE *WASA QUEEN* begins to thread her way through the scatter of rocks and islands lying south of Helsinki. She is bound for Tallinn, the capital of recently Soviet-free Estonia, three hours across the Gulf of Finland. Islands, some wooded and rounded like porcupines, others half-submerged and rocky, loll like submarines or seals off the Finnish port, creating a feeling of frivolity. This is not serious water, more a playful ante-room to the austere Baltic further east. Hydrofoils tow their boiling wakes as they cross and recross at high speed, teasing the white, top-heavy ferry ships on their more stately passages.

Helsinki waterfront, with its formal row of eighteenth-century port buildings, their ochre regularity broken only by the copper and gold spires of Gornostayer's Uspensky Orthodox church and the soaring white dome and turrets of the Lutheran cathedral, dwindles behind us, the funnels of tugs, the masts of fishing boats, the cluster of cranes, slipping out of sight until there is only the slightest of indentations to be descried. Soon even the gulls cease their flap and screech.

Tallinn had come to my notice a long time ago. After the German unconditional surrender in 1945 it was arranged that the task of redistributing the German fleet among the victorious Allies should be handed to the Royal Navy. The German ships, ordered back to their various home ports from wherever they happened to be, ended up at Wilhelmshaven, Bremen, Hamburg and Kiel, an assortment of battleships, cruisers, destroyers, minesweepers, E-boats and submarines. When the quotas were agreed the idea was that German crews would sail their own ships under surveillance to ports in America, Britain and the Soviet Union, returning as passengers to Germany.

There was an immediate setback, for the first ship, 2521, to be returned under this operation, one of a draft destined for the Soviet Union, docked at Tallinn, its crew guaranteed safe conduct home. They were never seen again.

Not surprisingly, German captains showed no enthusiasm for following them, threatening to scuttle their ships rather than take them to a Soviet port. It was arranged, therefore, that in future ships would sail under sealed orders, commanded by a British naval officer, but with their German crew intact. Their destination would be revealed only when well out at sea. Once handed over, their crews would return home in ships of the Royal Navy.

That was the theory anyway. TS19 had sailed from Bremerhaven at 0900 under the command, as far as internal matters were concerned, of Korvetten-Kapitän Schlemmer; Peter Döblin, with whom I had been at school, was First Lieutenant. As we approached the roads west of the Kiel Canal my yeoman of signals clattered on to the bridge with an envelope. I knew before I opened it what it would say. We had cleared the crew off the ship before sailing and a thorough search of all decks and cabins had been made as an insurance against sabotage.

Schlemmer had gone below to his cabin just after we passed Heligoland on our port beam. Heligoland had been a U-boat base, but it was destroyed in one terrifying night attack by Mitchell bombers. As we closed on it the rock openings that housed the U-boats were clearly visible. It had been a holiday island once, now scarcely inhabited.

I knocked on Schlemmer's door and when he held it

half-open a shape on his bunk was vaguely discernible. "You have company," I inquired, "perhaps I might be introduced?" He appeared unconcerned, but muttered something over his shoulder. Reluctantly, the shape disentangled itself from its protective sheeting to reveal an attractive girl in her early twenties, rather grubby, and wearing only pants. She was Polish, a dockyard worker who had prevailed upon Schlemmer, whom she knew, to let her stowaway to wherever we might be destined.

I gave Schlemmer the news and also a raised eyebrow. "I cannot answer for my crew," he replied, "for they lost many friends on our sister ship, but of course I will comply with your orders."

"You must answer for your crew," I said, "because it is my responsibility to see this ship is handed over intact to the Russians and if it is not you will be for the high jump. And I too, probably."

We had a couple of armed marines on board, but if the German crew had taken it into their heads to scuttle the ship or overpower us, there was little we could do except shoot a few of them. I'm not sure whether either marine had ever fired a gun in anger and they looked as unsuitable agents of destruction as the guns themselves. Meanwhile, I gave the order to alter course to starboard.

We had been on a dissembling, roundabout route that had taken us out into the North Sea as far as Sylt in the Friesian Islands. Sylt is almost entirely composed of sand dunes, in which both the wealthier and poorer classes, at opposite ends of the island, had been accustomed to loll naked during the golden months in happier days. Döblin had often been there with his family and had tales of mountainous women and their vast, insect-bitten arses. He and his brother used to hide in the long grasses and spy on the better-looking ones, until, one day, so absorbed in their research, they failed to notice a huge brute of a fellow who descended on them from behind and gave them a beating.

We slowed down, the change in engine revolutions causing the same adrenalin increase as it had rarely failed to do on patrol during the war. There were some noises, indicators of potential danger, that never lost their power to alarm.

Good sense, fortunately, had prevailed. Schlemmer called his ship's company together, pointing out the cost of an injudicious insurrection, most likely a long spell inside, and emphasising the presence of British warships in the Baltic, stationed as guarantees of safety in the area of likely ports of disembarkation.

From then on, all went well. We inched through the canal, cleared Lübeck Bay, and made our way south of Bornholm into the Baltic. Two days later, near the island of Saaremaa, south-west of Tallinn, we kept a rendezvous with two destroyers, one Soviet and one British. The German crew was transferred to the British escort and a skeleton Russian crew took over TS19 with a great show of bossiness leading us into Tallinn harbour. The much relieved marines and I returned on a minesweeper in which I had served three years earlier.

That was then. Now, as we moved gently on a clear autumn afternoon across the Gulf, an accordion band playing and Finnish couples performing solemn waltzes and fox-trots in the saloon – I had incorrectly been led to suppose that the ships would be full of drunken Finns on their way to cheap Estonian liquor – I began to think again of "old" Schlemmer. "Old" now, of course, indeed dead, though when we first met in circumstances more uncongenial for him than for me he was far from old. I was twenty-four, and he was perhaps in his late thirties, a career sailor from a long established naval family. TS19 was his second command and not one that suggested further promotion. The way to glory in the German navy was via U-boats or capital ships, like the *Tirpitz*, or *Hipper*, whose name still sent shivers down my spine and whose officers I could still see in my mind's eye directing fire as she closed on *Onslow*, preparatory to finishing us off. Although Schlemmer had fashionable naval connections – Admiral Doenitz was one – he had evidently been regarded as lacking in political zeal, a competent enough seaman, but a man of rather sophisticated tastes and frivolous habits.

After our Baltic adventure Schlemmer returned to Hamburg, was denazified in the manner of the time, and demobilised. His family had property, and a printing business, in Lower Saxony, near Celle. I was at that time editing a magazine for naval forces in Germany and because his terms were good, and I liked and trusted him, it became possible to put some small business his way. He was inordinately grateful, as most German families, of whatever background, were on the bread line.

Richard Schlemmer was, in appearance at least, a ladies' man: good-looking in rather a caddish way, dark glossy hair *en brosse*, aquiline features. He never actually wore a monocle, but looked as if he might. He did, however, use a cigarette holder and but for rather doggily sincere brown eyes he could have been taken for a younger Conrad Veidt. He possessed a gold Fabergé cigarette case and he would tap it in actorish fashion when at a momentary loss.

There were many such moments for Germans in those bleak winters immediately after the war. Refugees, swathed up against the cold and pushing their worldly belongings in pathetic little handcarts, swarmed in from the east. The concept of war criminals floated over the heads of anyone engaged in political, military or administrative duties, and various underground movements, like Werewolf, continued to recruit in the illusion that Germany would soon be back on its

feet, and that their secreted hoards of arms, usually in the
mountains, could still come in useful.

Schlemmer was no sort of Nazi, but like most serving
officers he had at least nominal allegiance to the Party. Over
the period of our business dealings I learned that on his
mother's side there were Polish and Estonian connections
and that since the halting of the German push east and the
subsequent Russian sweep towards Berlin all news of them
had ceased.

I was able from time to time to make inquiries on his
behalf though progress was slow. The Polish girl who had
hidden in his cabin on board TS19 emerged not long afterwards in Hamburg as a dancer and singer who found
employment in one of the cabarets on the Reeperbahn. The
whole St Pauli area, with its vast shipyards, was little more
than rubble, but women with torches flitted about the ruins
like fireflies. The German songs of the moment, "*Abends in
der Kaserne*" and incongruously "*Es ist ein Frühling ohne
Ende*", could be heard drifting out of basements, and in the
Atlantic Hotel and the Vierjahreseiten Ilse Werner and Lala
Anderson murmured their throaty versions of "Lili Marlene"
for the thousandth time.

German officers like Schlemmer were allowed no part
of this. Whereas a year earlier high-spirited and glamorous
U-boat and destroyer officers held court at the Atlantic Bar
swigging champagne cocktails and brandy Alexanders, now
they were reduced to mere observers, their defeated and
hangdog expressions lightening at the merest civility.

By the time I was posted from Hamburg, and then from
Germany altogether, Schlemmer had begun to prosper. He
acquired an office near the Opera and sailed a boat on the
Alster. He wrote inviting me to make contact and dine
with him if I should visit Hamburg, and in due course,
researching articles for *Tribune* and later the *Observer*, I took

him up on his offer. We went to a swish club on the water's
edge and were joined by Ledig Rowohlt, whose father was
then the leading publisher in Germany and whom Ledig
succeeded.
Memories of war began to recede. Hamburg lost its smell
of death and decay and in almost miraculous fashion earlier
elegance became recognisable. Schlemmer wrote to say he
was now printing for Rowohlt and that he had married an
Estonian girl, the daughter of one of the families I had helped
him to trace. His future seemed set fair, in a faintly irritating
manner in comparison with the impoverished, badly fed and
coarsely clothed English of the time.

Over the years we met occasionally, in London or in Germany.
At a Frankfurt Book Fair he told me that he was no longer
involved in his own printing business, that he had taken
on a partner, a practising Nazi as he later discovered, who
had got the firm into trouble by printing neo-Nazi tracts,
as a consequence of which a lot of other work had been
lost. He was considering a move to Estonia, where his wife's
family had property in the town of Haapsalu. By now he
was in his late seventies, still sleek as an otter, slightly grey.
His daughter had chosen to earn a living in Estonia, being
fluent in Polish and Estonian as well as German and English,
and her language skills had become valuable to the Soviet
occupiers.
His move took place in 1990, shortly before the departure
of the Russians. I didn't imagine a German naval officer of
the Nazi period would have been particularly welcome in
a country that had suffered almost as much under the
Germans as under the Russians, though before the war more
than half of Estonia had been in the hands of German-Balt
families. In the various struggles for Estonia that succeeded
the Russian Revolution the Estonian nationalists, with secret

support from the Royal Navy, had finally defeated the Bolsheviks at Narva. A force of nearly 20,000 Bolsheviks was herded back into Russian territory and, not long after, the Russian occupiers moved out of Estonia, leaving thousands of disgruntled communists behind.

The Nazi–Soviet Pact of 1939 left the Soviet Union free to annex Estonia and Latvia, a consequence of which was the conscription of some 60,000 Estonians into the Soviet army, their deportation, and in many cases eventual execution. With the German invasion of 1941 the Estonians were able to compare the questionable benefits of life under the Nazis with life under the Russians. Such Jewish families as there were, far fewer than in Latvia and Lithuania, were soon murdered, but in 1944 the Russians were back, the German High Command in Tallinn surrendering to the Red Army on 22 September. By now Estonia was seriously depopulated, refugees streaming west or being rounded up and sent to Soviet labour camps. To all intents and purposes Estonia became a Soviet province, much as the Tsars had always envisaged. A local Soviet-led communist party took control, Russians using the country to establish factories and industrial sites close to their own borders. A German-orientated population now became heavily Russian.

In 1992 I heard again from Schlemmer. He was in poor health but happy to have seen the last of the Russians. He had shed his German nationality as easily as a snake its skin, and was becoming coherent in the Finno-Ugric Estonian language as well as the Russian generally practised in shops and offices. He had taken up yoga and was studying Buddhism, recommending to me the works of the Estonian poet Jaan Kaplinski, some of whose lines he sent me in translation. Kaplinski's poetry seemed to be motivated by a close scrutiny of the countryside surrounding his home in Tartu, where he taught at the university. Schlemmer, a former disciple of Ernst Jünger, had taken to going on long solitary walks and, according to his wife, had become a mystic. I was never quite sure what she meant by this because soon after I last spoke to her she died.

The next time I heard anything about Schlemmer was in a call from his daughter. There had been some difficulties with the Russians over what were alleged to be activities by Schlemmer on behalf of the German government. Through his wife Schlemmer had acquired complicated Polish-Estonian connections, which, added to his own mixed parentage, gave him conflicting loyalties in an already muddled and shifting political situation. He had suffered a heart attack and was in hospital in Tallinn. I learned inadvertently from this telephone call that the woman in Schlemmer's cabin in TS19 all those years ago was no ordinary dockyard worker but a partly Jewish relative whose appearance had mercifully disguised her origins. She, too, had retired to Tallinn and had a daughter who was reputed to be an actress of sorts.

I had long contemplated a visit to Schlemmer in his newly acquired persona as family mystic and had a lingering curiosity about the Baltic coastline we had sailed along, Schlemmer and I side by side on the bridge, to our Russian rendezvous. In 1994, on a coastal steamer from Gdansk to Gdynia, I was reminded of those days by that particularly Baltic smell, a fusion of salt, sand dunes, pine trees and tar.

Had I known it, Schlemmer was already in final decline, a letter on my return from his daughter saying he was not expected to leave hospital. Nor did he, being buried in the Forest Cemetery at Kloostrimetsa.

I regretted not making my visit in time to see him once more, for he was a curious part of my wartime past which, for one reason or another, lingered on. He had, as a German naval officer of pre-war vintage, known good times, riding high on professional and political illusions he never really had his heart in. But his background and family network were not without ambiguities and his whole career was symptomatic of that of many professional German families whose relations, interests and connections had strayed outside the confines of the Third Reich. He survived the bad times, but there were concealed elements that gave a nervous edge to his post-war existence. During the time in the late 1940s, when I had an interest in the movements of Nazi war criminals, he was of discreet assistance to me and I was happy to be of some use to him in smoothing out family and other arrangements during a period when formidable bureaucratic obstacles were put in the way of the most harmless of requests.

I had expected the Gulf of Finland, where a few years earlier a ferry had capsized, to be choppy if not rough. Instead, it was like glass, the endless slivers of land, rock, lighthouse reflected clearly back on it. Now that I was belatedly making the long-intended pilgrimage, out of curiosity perhaps more than piety, though with the thought of laying a few flowers on Schlemmer's grave, I began to realize I knew virtually nothing about the country whose thin coastline like a squeeze of toothpaste lay ahead.

Arthur Ransome, to judge from his book *Recundra's First Cruise,* had played some part in negotiating the independence of Estonia, having palled up with Lenin. They became keen opponents at chess and in 1919 Ransome had a boat designed for himself in Tallinn. "Reval", as the city was called until 1917, was built as a fortress on a rock, and, Ransome wrote, "from the rock one looks out over a wide bay, with the green wooded island of Nargon on one side of it, a long promontory on the other, and far out beyond the bay a horizon of open sea. I do not believe that a man can look out from that rock and ever be wholly happy until he has got a boat of his own. I could not."

Not sharing Ransome's and his wife Eugenia's enthusiasm

for sailing – she had been a secretary to Trotsky – I needed to look elsewhere for literary enlightenment. My friend Jeremy Lewis reminded me of references to Estonia in Graham Greene's *Ways of Escape,* which I had looked up. They were pretty sketchy, but he had sometime in the thirties received a letter marked only *Poste Restante* from the Norwegian writer Nordahl Grieg, a rather glamorous figure who was shot down over Berlin in 1943. "I assure you," Grieg had written, "that you before or later must come to Estonia, and please come now. It is a charming country, absolutely unspoilt, and the cheapest in the world. I am a very poor author, but here I can afford everything – a strange and marvellous feeling. If the weather is good, do let us hire a sailing boat and go for a week among the islands. The population there has scarcely seen a white man before, and for a few pieces of chocolate we could certainly buy what native girls we wanted to. Do come."

It seemed an enticing offer, but Greene at the time was too poor to take it up. Nordahl Grieg was someone who had caught my imagination during patrols off Norway in 1943, Norwegian officers speaking reverently about him.

However, Greene did in due course visit Estonia "for no good reason", as he writes, "except escape to somewhere new". He flew in from Riga in a small plane in which there were only two passengers. Both turned out, in somewhat unlikely fashion, to be reading Henry James "in the same small Macmillan edition".

His fellow passenger was a former armaments salesman, in earlier life an Anglican clergyman who had converted to Catholicism, now installed as British consul at Tallinn. The consul was a bachelor with time on his hands, so the two spent many happy hours together, Greene records, "when I was not vainly searching for a brothel which had been run by the same family in the same house for three hundred years". His informant had been Baroness Budberg, former mistress of Gorky, Bruce Lockhart and H.G. Wells, whose views on such a subject were likely to be authoritative.

Towards the end of her life, when she was lonely and encamped in the Cromwell Road, not far from my office, I saw Moura Budberg on almost a weekly basis. Her entertaining, helped along by various Russian acolytes, was now much reduced, but her invitations were peremptory. Any excuses – that one was going to the theatre, the cinema, the ballet or simply working – were brushed aside as if of no account. "Just come in for a little moment", she would wheedle in her husky voice, which remained distinctive and seductive long after all other physical charms had fled and she had become heavily square in shape.

Her directions appeared to have been inadequate, for Greene, despite dogged attempts, failed to find the house. Asking the help of a waiter in Tallinn's leading hotel, he was told politely: "There is nothing of that kind which we cannot arrange for you here."

Greene does not confirm accepting such an offer. He makes no reference to a single building in Tallinn, or stretch of countryside, nor to any one of the many beautiful churches. Tallinn, to him, seems to have been just background for talk with his new friend. "For a fortnight, thanks to Henry James, we were close friends. Afterwards? I never knew what happened. He must have lost his homes when the Russians moved in. It seemed hardly a danger in those days – our eyes were on Germany." There was also a bonus, for thirty years later a parcel of Henry James first editions arrived in the post – a present from the now eighty-year-old ex-armaments-dealer, Anglican clergyman and Catholic convert, "thus crowning one of the most pleasant chance encounters of my life".

Colin Thubron in his book *Among the Russians* describes an equally unlikely seeming literary encounter in Tallinn's old market square. "I saw a man with *To the Lighthouse* sticking out of one pocket and made it an excuse for conversation." Virginia Woolf to an Estonian must have been quite something.

Thubron shook the dust of Estonia from his feet even more rapidly than Greene had done, but the few pages he devotes to Tallinn evoke the feel of the city in a manner not attempted by the brothel-hunting Greene. Thubron was driving west from Leningrad and on the way into Estonia gave a lift to a hitch-hiking student of archaeology from Tartu University. In a campsite at Tallinn Thubron finds himself among a rowdy crowd of Estonians on holiday from parts of Scandinavia. "Released from the restrictive Finnish drinking laws they celebrated into the night in a long, free uproar, while the Soviet Estonians sat dourly round their primus stoves, frying lumps of fish and boiling semolina." This was in the early 1980s. I did not have the impression in Helsinki of any significant restriction in drinking times, but the poet Herbert Lomas, who taught there for some years, confirmed the strictness of bars about allowing entry to anyone who was apparently under the influence of anything stronger than beer. "You've been tasting," the manager would say, shutting the door firmly on the unfortunate. Lomas had a friend with prominent teeth whose expression tended to suggest a permanent, rather idiotic grin. As a consequence he was frequently and unjustly turned away from drinking places with the stern admonishment, "You've been tasting!"

Even in 1983, when Estonia was still a Soviet republic, Thubron was able to comment on the leftover feeling of war at the same time remarking on how life appeared better and freer than anywhere else in the Soviet Union. Thubron's Woolf-reading friend elaborated on the theme of Russian immigration, of how with the development of Baltic industry – heavy engineering and chemicals – hordes of Russians arrived to fill the jobs. "They lived in great apartment blocks, dirtily, like pigs. They had money, but spent it on drink."

The Woolf-reader turned out to be a chemist and a Methodist, non-smoking, non-drinking. It was only in Estonia, apparently, that Methodism had survived at all in the Soviet Union, and then only among the very young and the very old. The Stalin generation was conspicuous by its absence.

Later, in the Methodist headquarters near the market square, Thubron came on an ancient pastor who had been to sea as a young man when Tsar Nicholas II was still on the throne. He had worked on a Yarmouth-bound clipper and been converted to Methodism by a nurse in an Oslo hospital after his ship had caught fire. There was not much left for him these days, only God, and God had not been much in evidence for a long time now.

In 1989 I had published in *London Magazine* an article by Ian Thomson called "Sailing to Tallinn". Thomson's mother had been born in Estonia, but had escaped before the arrival of the Red Army. Anticipating his first visit to the country, Thomson wrote to Greene inquiring about his reasons for changing the original setting of what came to be called *Our Man in Havana*. Greene replied, "The reason why I changed the setting from Estonia to Cuba was that one could hardly sympathize with the main character if he was to be involved in the Hitler war. I already knew Cuba and the Fidelistas in the mountains . . . I am afraid I saw very little of Estonia apart from Tallinn and have very little memories of the place except that it had a great charm for me."

Thomson called on the Estonian legation in South Kensington before setting out, the building run single-handedly by a Mrs Anna Taru. "The first thing I want to tell you," she had said to him, "is that I do not hate the Russians. Many of them would give you their last piece of bread. It

is the Communists we Estonians cannot abide." From South
Kensington that seemed a reasonable distinction, though not
one many in Estonia today seem inclined to make, nor those
Ian Thomson met in his turn. The legation has since closed.

I was glad to read Thomson's piece again on the voyage over,
as now – the city coming into close focus – I was able with his
help to identify some of the buildings in this "oriental city of
minarets and knitting-needle spires, of churches obelisk-
high". That tallest of Gothic spires, copper-covered and
sharpened pencil-shape, must be St Olaf, a fourteenth-century
landmark for navigators, which, as Ian suggested, probably
guided Nelson on his way from the Battle of Copenhagen
to attack the Russian fleet anchored in the Bay of Tallinn.
"A small town resembling a large fortress" was the description
of the Arab traveller Abdu Mohamed Idris arriving here in the
twelfth century and certainly, the nearer we got, it seemed apt.

It is a skyline one couldn't forget: in the afternoon the
wreath of green enfolding the tilted cluster of tiled buildings,
spires and towers breaking out as if from surf, and nearer
the water's edge the frieze of cranes in mid-pirouette like a
frenetic *corps de ballet*, the bloated white shapes of the ferries,
the nosing tugs. At sunset, dark starting to wash out the
details, the sky floods, water light curdled with oil, the skyline
jagged and feverish. It was this night skyline that Andrew
Grieve's recent film *Letter from the East* made indelible.

Grieve's film, about the confusion during the Soviet
take-over of Tallinn when parents were separated from their
children and thousands were herded off to Siberia, their fate
never known, reminded me of Schlemmer and the situation
of the Estonian side of his family. In one of his letters to me,
when he knew his days were numbered, he gave me a list of
addresses in Tallinn where his relatives and friends had lived.
"They'll probably all be dead by the time you get here, if you

ever do, but it might amuse you over an afternoon to look
their hovels out." General Mihailovitch, when he knew he had
lost out to Tito's partisans for Allied support during the
1939–45 war, admitted ruefully that he and his men "had
been caught up in the gale of the world". Estonia had suffered
in this gale more than most. A century earlier, as recon-
structed in Jaan Kross's great novel set in Alexander's Russia
of the 1820s, *The Tsar's Madman,* even those most in the
confidence of the Tsar himself were subjected to constant
scrutiny by police informers, friend set against friend. Kross
himself, most renowned of living Estonian novelists, had
been deported to Siberia in 1946, spending eight years in
the Gulag before being allowed to return to Tallinn to write
novels and poetry, and translate from the languages studied
in detention.

Germans are customarily and properly identified as the
authors of other people's dispossession. As a German,
Schlemmer, in his turn, had to suffer silently in witness of
his own relatives' misfortunes at Russian hands in a country
with shifting identities.

The Russian suburbs, whose apartment blocks stretch like
giant tombstones to the east of the port, reminded me that
this was the nearest I had got to Murmansk since I had
suffered, in the battered *Onslow* after an Arctic convoy, the
playful but regular bombing by trainee German pilots from
their nearby base in Finland. Luckily, they were inaccurate.
Soviet Russia for most of one's life has suggested gloom,
corruption and threat, and the sight of these extraordinary,
glacial edifices, rising with their hundreds of slit eyes out of
unlandscaped ground, was not promising. But though their
surgical and austere functionalism, making no concessions
to any idea of the good life, caught the eye further out to
sea than Tallinn itself, it was not towards them, but to a small

wooded hump, its spires like hedgehog quills, that we slowly steamed. As we came alongside, one or two bleary-looking Finns did emerge from the lower saloons, but they stumbled harmlessly along the quay to the cheap, by Finnish standards, liquid delights ahead of them. It was no longer Soviet soil that we disembarked on, for which I was grateful. The last time I had done so, going ashore to the Red Cross canteen at Vianga not so far to the north, our gallant Russian allies used to amuse themselves by taking pot shots at us. Perhaps in our fur hats and coats they thought we were bears. Vianga, in the Kola inlet, is now the largest site of unstable nuclear material in the world.

The port at Tallinn is a modest affair, a widish bay, in which the ferries reverse to go in stern first, narrowing to two quays, for freight and passengers, blocked off on the land side by a terminal building resembling a railway carriage. But soon, above the narrow apron of woods that separates the modern town from old Tallinn, there were reassuring glimpses of copper and gold, vestiges of a civilization far removed from the one suggested by the featureless tenements behind us.

I wondered how Schlemmer, nearing the end of his life, had felt about finishing up in this once German, then Soviet-run city. It was not a great distance from here, after all, that he had been obliged in humiliating circumstances to hand over his ship to Russian sailors he would have thought his inferiors. They were not much to my taste either, for in 1942, despite an agreement that they would meet the convoys and escort them into Archangel, they rarely turned up, pleading rough weather, thereby giving our destroyers tedious extra days to the White Sea.

For professional sailors of good family, the intrusion of Nazism into an orderly, seagoing life must have required a crude silencing of instincts. The price they subsequently paid, if not with their lives, had in Schlemmer's case to be paid twice, as with all German families rooted in the east. When he decided to pack up and retire to Estonia, he was not to know that the days of Soviet occupation were numbered. Many of his mother's and wife's relatives had disappeared into thin air and now he was re-entering, willingly, what was to him the zone of infamy. "I am returning to nowhere from somewhere," he had written to me, "perhaps like Nabokov I shall take up the study of butterflies or like Kaplinski engage with forests. You must read him."

A later, hurried scrawl, describing his exploration of Tallinn before he set out for his new home off Matsalu Bay, did much to reassure me that all would not be lost for him. "It is a magical city," he wrote, "Tsarist in imagination, German Lutheran in detail. I could be at home here if I had anyone left that mattered." I would, in due course, follow some of his descriptions to the letter. But familiarising myself with the medieval city, many of its buildings half-collapsed and almost beyond repair, I could not help but feel that for Schlemmer it must have evoked memories of Hamburg or Bremen, with pockets of occupiers still holding out and conversing in a secret language. Most people need to feel that somewhere for them is home, but for eastern Europeans, Germans, Balts or Slavs, who have been tilted first one way then another, the very notion must seem like a mirage. English villagers, whether through immigration or the influx of city workers, often now feel a minority in their places of birth, steadily becoming unrecognisable to them, but in places like Estonia, where one imposed dreaded language is succeeded by another and their own Finno-Ugric speech is at a discount, it must be a hundred times worse.

Although Russian had inevitably become the common language of the people, there were enough German speakers about should Schlemmer have felt homesick. It was noticeable even now that in certain places only Russian was acknowledged, and in others German. Not only in speech does the Russian presence hang over the city, for thousands of Russian workers, left over after the departure of their soldiers, and other Russian-speaking local communists, ensure a brooding, occasionally surfacing, sourness. It is the more disconcerting when one comes across it, for despite the inevitable conflicts of loyalty among people occupied almost permanently by foreign powers the Estonians have struggled historically, against all odds, to retain an identity of their own.

Tallinn, as I began to explore it, revealed itself as compact and self-contained, the Old Town or *Vanalinn,* compressed within a handsome sixteenth-century wall decorated by forty-eight towers. The wall, in surprisingly good repair, is breached by eight, evenly spaced gates. Encircling the wall, separating the Old Town from its modern extension, gently drifting waters of a moat, bordered by swathes of succulent green, in turn give way to tree-lined boulevards. The effect is of a series of tight, concentric circles, to the centre of which, from anywhere on the circumference, is a matter of minutes. Time and again, unsure of my bearings, I entered the nearest gate to find myself within sight of Raekoja Plats, the main square, and my hotel. I had been well advised to book in at the only hotel within the fortifications, which although it had no outlook except blank walls across a narrow street and no restaurant, was uniquely placed. The girls at reception were flirtatious, pretty, tall and fair in the manner of many younger Estonian women, though a Russian-looking bruiser lurked permanently in the background. Only Estonian money, kroons or eeks, was acceptable, the handing-over of which lent a curiously surreptitious air to transactions habitually conducted by credit card or cheque.

Raekoja Plats, a large, cobbled square, slightly tilted, is at the centre of city affairs. The drab, early fifteenth-century

Town Hall, in the manner of a Gothic barn, weighs the square down at one end, despite an incongruously perched biscuit-coloured steeple that hosts a copper weathervane. For a German arriving to live here there must have been something comforting about the steep, narrow streets, the cobbled alleyways, the uniformity of the pastel-coloured buildings, all of roughly the same vintage as the Town Hall. While I was there, repainting was under way, dark greys, olive greens, navy blues, pale pinks and pistachio, masking the elegant austerity of the merchants' houses, pharmacies and shops that line the square. There are outdoor cafés on the northern side, and from one of these Schlemmer had sent me a postcard on which he had written, "God knows what I have let myself in for, Russians everywhere, tanks, and my Estonian relatives, some of them better viewed from a distance. There are, though, some beauties about."

I thought sometimes that the city was like a great, iced confection crumbling at the edges, frivolous on the surface, but sober and grave underneath. Whichever way you looked, there was something to catch and please the eye, a dome here, a spire there, the Gothic and the baroque adjacent, and handsome guild houses bearing coats of arms over their porticos sliding down to sea level off Raekoja Plats.

From the Upper Town, Toompea, you can look out over the wide, forested shore of the Bay of Tallinn, the docks with their cranes and shipping and, immediately below, in a horseshoe, the tiled roofs of the Lower Town. A ruff of trees gives a kind of nesting quality to the city's alignment.

Toompea was the site of the original Estonian settlement and it was here that the top brass, ecclesiastical and feudal, settled, with the business and craft areas developing lower down. From my hotel I could reach Toompea's castle square by way of the almost vertical Pikk Jalg (Long Leg) in a few minutes, the view at the top stunning in all directions. The spruce and elegant pink palace that houses the present parliament suffers in scale and restraint from the bulbous exoticism of Alexander Nevsky Cathedral, but juxtaposed over the foaming parks below they show off Tallinn's brilliant duality. In 1989 the Chain of Freedom, a Baltic demonstration – a veritable human chain – against Russian occupation, which stretched over 400 miles to Vilnius in Lithuania, started out on Linda's Hill near the square, Estonians, Latvians, Lithuanians linking hands in what became known as the Singing Revolution.

Someone with one leg longer than the other would get on well in Tallinn's Upper Town, for there is nothing not on a steep slope. One or other of the eleven bells of Alexander Nevsky seems permanently to be ringing, while outside on the square bundled-up peasant women cross themselves and await offerings. The interior walls, in a jagged olive, red and white, resemble the camouflage zig-zag that used to be painted on warships. The singing is memorable, the poorest of the poor affectingly prostrating themselves in thanks for precious little, one imagined.

There are other churches in Toompea, notably the Lutheran Dome Church, a charcoal-coloured Gothic building of the thirteenth century, but a sense of isolated magnificence prevails, the wind gusting through propped-up wood houses and scudding clouds showing through holed roofs. History has passed on, or is perhaps taking a breather, in these once heavily guarded and sacred precincts. A few gun emplacements and fortified towers, aimlessly surveying Kopli Bay to the north, are all that is left.

In one of his erratic postcards Schlemmer had once scrawled, "You and I saw enough cemeteries fifty years ago to last a lifetime, but there is one here you should see. It is more a forest than a graveyard, the corpses so discreetly submerged in leaves that they seem mainly there to provide mulch."

So, one sunny autumn morning, I picked up the 34 tram outside the Central Post Office on Narva Mnt Metsakalnistu (the Forest Cemetery) lies some miles along a wide seaside road, flanked with oleanders, palms and other flowering trees of the kind you would find somewhere like Bordighera or Rapallo. It follows the curve of the wide bay, with yachts bobbing off club jetties to seaward and on the inland side the informal, country-like woods and fields of Kadriorg Park, designed in honour of Peter the Great's wife Catherine by Niccolo Michetti in the early years of the eighteenth century.

This whole area has a gentle, civilized feel to it, its bene- volence brought to an abrupt and brutal halt by the Soviet- built estate at Lasnamae. The Russians, having conceived the place, proceeded to fill it with immigrant fellow countrymen, to an extent that it became known as "Little Leningrad". Its incongruity is all the more striking in that the surrounding area consists of neighbourhood allotments and suburban villas, neatly aligned in their wooded avenues.

The road to the Forest Cemetery turns off the marine highway, but before it does so you pass the two curiously affecting memorials, one called the Russalka Memorial, consisting of a wrecked granite ship, a bronze angel on its masthead. In 1893 the *Russalka* had sunk just off the bay with the loss of 170 Russian sailors. The Soviets erected on the other side of the highway an elaborate complex of obelisks, archways and headstones dedicated to the 1917 revolution and the Tallinn divisions of what they called the Great Patriotic War 1944–5. There, too, is the grave of the sailor Yvgeny Nikolov, murdered by the Nazis. The Soviets may have departed politically and spiritually, but there is no shortage of reminders of their presence. I wondered how long the Estonians would put up with them.

The tram stops outside the cemetery gates and before you

lie hundreds of silver birches and pines on raised terraces as orderly as soldiers on parade. Gardeners potter about turning over the rich soil for new customers, and the graves themselves lie shadowy and discreet under branches, their headstones covered with lichen.

I knew I would never find Schlemmer's grave for there are thousands stretching over many acres. There are German names galore, Russians, Swedes, whole avenues devoted to "Sporting Heroes", and a hill of "Celebrities". Poli-Ann and May Poldar, Alex Kurritsa and Maria Teichmann lie side by side and though the cemetery – one of seven in Tallinn, including a Jewish one – was opened only in 1933 there have been enough casualties of every race since then to make wounding inroads into the forest.

It is a soothing and tranquil place, the human no longer intrusive, the dead at rest. I had gone once with Schlemmer to a German naval cemetery outside Hamburg, sailors' insignia and caps laid like flowers on the graves, and he had pointed out old ship mates, with tears in his eyes. There were no evident signs of soldiery here, but if there had been the dappled light and drifting leaves would have hidden them. Cathedrals, they talk about, but in the naves of these thin tree-trunks, like the legs of grey racehorses, there is not so much gloom as armistice, a reunion of enemies several times removed, tranquillized under a Baltic ceiling.

Back up Viru Street, with its flower stalls and old women selling tatty fur coats and hats, and along Rataskaevu Street, with its tiny theatre and winking *Non-Stop Striptease* sign opposite – the fanciful idea came to me that some descendant of the Polish stowaway might be performing there – to my hotel, where I began to read Arthur Ransome's autobiography. About his sailing enthusiasms and about his *Swallows and Amazons* and other children's books I knew, but

I had no idea of the extraordinary life he had led earlier, his long drawn-out association with Russia during and after the Revolution, his time in Tallinn, not only sailing but to a large extent brokering Estonian independence.

It was in 1913 that Ransome, then twenty-nine, made his first visit to Russia, arriving at St Petersburg by steamer via Copenhagen and Stockholm. These waters were ones he was soon to be familiar with in a series of small boats. On the steamer he heard from a fellow passenger the Russian expression used for a sudden break in conversation, "A policeman is being born," surely apter for our century than "An angel is passing."

Ransome, already the author of a book on Oscar Wilde, was keen to gather material for a collection of stories based on Russian folklore. He wanted to learn the language and to escape from a miserable marriage. The British fleet was in St Petersburg, and Ransome, commissioned by Douglas Goldring to write a short guide to the city, had a good time. A love affair with Russia was begun, only to be interrupted by the outbreak of war. Ransome returned home by steamer, evading German destroyers off North Cape by following much the same route I was to take in the minesweeper *Harrier* thirty years later.

Extreme short-sight had ruled out military service for Ransome, but he was soon back in Russia, Moscow this time, with vague journalistic commissions. Hugh Walpole was installed there trying to learn Russian and they became friends.

In due course, Ransome was made the *Daily News* correspondent in Russia, his predecessor having collapsed on the job.

The war, in progress now for over a year, was not going well for the ill-armed Russians, and correspondents were not welcome at the Front. Nevertheless, within a few months,

Ransome had worked his way down to Kiev and into Galicia, where the Russian and Austrian armies had so muddled themselves up that patrols frequently wandered by mistake into enemy trenches.

Before any of his newspaper colleagues concerned themselves, Ransome took an interest in the Soviet of Soldiers' and Workers' Deputies and acquired a more realistic view of the possibilities. "In the excitement of the revolution I did for a few days allow myself to think that the army would get, as it were, a second wind and, re-armed with revolutionary fervour, emulate the armies of Napoleon and carry all before it. But I very soon saw that though this might eventually happen it would not happen now, and, all through that summer of 1917 I, like every Russian I knew, was watching for any sign that the war might end before the Russian collapse that seemed to me inevitable . . . It was obvious that the Soviets held what power there was, and that the Duma was an impotent anachronism. The story of 1917 is the story of the demonstration of that all-important fact."

Ransome's faith in the peasant soldier as the hero of spontaneous revolution resulted in his sending home a telegram in which he wrote, "The few simple soldiers in Petrograd who refused to fire on their fellows struck in two days the fetters from their nation. This is far and away the greatest victory over Prussianism gained in this war. A red flag of revolution is flying over the Winter Palace."

Although the Kerensky government was soon to fall and the Bolsheviks would assume a majority, Ransome was detached enough to report back that neither the Bolshevik nor the Kerensky government represented the majority of Russians, "because the majority of Russians do not care one way or the other. The majority would acquiesce in anything that should give them bread, peace and some sort of order."

While the war and the power struggle continued on their

various paths Ransome, as the most influential foreign correspondent, was mixing with the top officials of both sides. Visiting Trotsky at the Smolny Institute, he became attracted to his secretary, Evgenia, an attraction that over the next turbulent months developed into a love affair that lasted for the rest of his life.

The Germans meanwhile, declining the request made by Lenin and Trotsky for renewed negotiations, continued to advance. Ransome found himself helping to pack the Imperial Archives, the Government having decided to move from Petrograd to Moscow. In July 1918, the Tsar and his family were murdered at Ekaterinburg and the Allied embassies moved north to Archangel.

With the German armies now in as bad a state as the Russians, there was nothing to keep the war going. Ransome was able to work on his never realised history of the Revolution, in the meantime gaining material for his *Six Weeks in Russia in 1919,* a report on conditions and characters that would be made available to a not much interested Foreign Office. Ransome was able to talk and discuss with most of the great men of the time, almost all in the end murdered: Bukharin, Rykov, Zinoviev, Vorovsky, Trotsky. But his views about the folly of Intervention made him unpopular with our own Foreign Office and ineffectual steps were taken to arrest him. On his return he was summoned to report to the head of Scotland Yard and to explain his politics. Having spelled out the reasons as to why British interference in Russian affairs would do lasting damage whichever side won, he was alarmed to discover that plans were already in process for the financing and equipping of the Whites for large-scale civil war.

With Evgenia trapped in Russia and himself denied visas to return, Ransome spent the summer of 1919 fishing, trying not to imagine the worst. By luck and endless effort he was able, despite a coal strike bringing most shipping to a standstill, finally to get a passage on a Norwegian freighter bound for Bergen. From there he travelled by train to Stockhom, where the Estonian steamer *Kalevipoeg* was about to sail for Reval (Tallinn). "She was in some need of paint. She had no heating. Her decks leaked. But she moved, and brought me at last into the harbour of Reval, with the old castle on its rock looking out over the bay. The news I heard there was grim. General Judenitch had advanced and his forward troops were already within sight of the gilded dome of St Isaac's Cathedral in Petrograd."

The rest of my time in Tallinn was spent largely in the ghostly company of the bald man with walrus whiskers. Photographs show Ransome at the time to resemble Kipling, though as he grew stouter, and better set up, he became more like Conan Doyle. Ransome had lived through the Revolution, an apolitical observer with no axe to grind, and his reflections on the bizarre situation of a small Baltic country pushed round like a piece of meat on a dog's plate could only make the towers and cupolas, the cracked stone and rotten wood, all round me take on new interest. Tallinn is a lived-in city, the marks of its experiences vividly evident on its walls.

It was after Ransome's return to the city in 1919 that his involvement with it, and his influence on Estonian affairs, properly developed. Estonia's independence, following on the collapse of Germany, was precarious, with a White Russian army based on Reval and Judenitch threatening to deal with "the potato republic" once he had disposed of the Bolsheviks. His tanks, many of them commanded by British officers, were halted only when the British were replaced by Russians.

At this stage, with Estonia longing for Judenitch's defeat but fearful of the consequences, Ransome was asked by the sweetly named Foreign Minister, Mr Piip, to act as a go-between with the Soviets. His return to Moscow in fulfilment

of this mission more than once nearly led to Ransome being
shot as a spy. He survived, met Lenin and Litvinov, and was
reunited with Evgenia. However, the Bolsheviks were as
reluctant to open formal negotiations, as were the Estonians,
for fear that this would be treated as a sign of weakness.
In a few weeks, nevertheless, both sides overcame their reser-
vations and by the time Ransome reported back to Mr Piip a
peace treaty was being worked out that would safeguard
Estonia's independence. It was to last until the signing of the
Nazi–Soviet Pact of 1939. When years later Ransome encountered Mr Piip at a party, the former Foreign Minister took him
aside, confiding, "I have been going through our archives of
1919–1920 and I should like to tell you that you have a very
honourable place in Estonian history."

Ransome made several more incursions into Russia, now
on behalf of the *Manchester Guardian,* but he was excused
further meddling in politics. On his second honeymoon he
went sailing in the Baltic; he bought for £10 an unprepossessing boat that was being painted on the beach and which
he christened *Slug.* It had a mast and two ancient sails. On
their first night out the Ransomes were woken at dawn by
a loud barking. "I thought we must have drifted ashore while
we slept. The dawn had come. I looked sleepily over the
gunwale into the eyes of a large seal who, with shining head
and dripping whiskers, might have been an elderly business
man, bathing at Margate. He blew through his whiskers,
barked again, dived, and was gone."

Slug provided Mrs Ransome with an initiation into sailing,
but the boat sank twice at her moorings and finally, in Tallinn
harbour, had her compass and mainsail stolen. For the rest of
their lives the Ransomes were never without a boat.

They had no better luck with their next purchase, made
in Tallinn after a visit to Russia, in 1921. This they called
Kittiwake, 16 feet overall and top-heavy. Tallinn had no

boatbuilders so they had to call on an undertaker to knock
up a dinghy.

Kittiwake's keenness to capsize led to more ambitious plans.
An out-of-work German boat designer whom they met agreed
to design a proper boat for them, one in which they could live
and if necessary sail to England. They named the boat
Racundra, and about their adventures in it Ransome wrote
one of his most successful children's book, *Racundra's First
Cruise,* published in 1923.

In *Racundra* the Ransomes sailed the Finnish islands,
returning to Tallinn during the pike-run. "Here, in the gulf,
pike behave like salmon. In the winter when the streams are
frozen, they go, like the salmon, to the sea, and in the spring
they come up the streams to spawn, such of them as evade
the humans who are waiting for them with spears, traps and
nets, to make golden caviare of their roe and to dry good
white fillets of pike-flesh in the sun. When the pike-run is on,
you may see the pike alive in tubs in Reval market, and watch
a housewife carrying one home still kicking in her shopping
basket."

After Lenin's death in 1924 Stalin, the Communist Party
secretary, edged out of the shadows, and Ransome's long
involvement with Estonia and Russian politics came to an end.
Racundra, after a final leisurely cruise among the narrow,
reed-bordered channels of the Dvina, was laid up for the last
time. Ransome's divorce from his first wife came through and
"the Master of *Racundra* was married to the Cook at the British
Consulate in Reval".

It was salutary reading about Ransome, Estonia and the
Revolution now that the worst seemed once more to be over.
From the ramparts of Toompea one could look out over the
waters sailed by *Slug* and *Racundra*, now glassy in a week of
calm autumn weather. Ransome put a lot of his sailing
experience in Baltic waters into the children's books he spent

the rest of his life writing. For him Tallinn was a port as much as a city, though he spent many happy months in a hotel called the Golden Lion, which no longer seems to exist. I had come as a wartime sailor to these parts, witness of equally dramatic historic events, the consequences of which were to affect others of my acquaintance more than me. But reading Ransome's book and learning more about the early history of Tallinn made me see recent events in a longer perspective. After my 1945 voyage with Schlemmer in TS19 I wrote a long story about our journey into the Baltic and kept it in an old Kriegsmarine file for more than thirty years. When I moved from Sussex to London in 1978 the musty smell of its pages, the German ribbon it was tied up in, no longer suggested usefulness. Along with surviving remnants of those days – an RNVR officer's jacket with the gold braid hanging loose, a German Admiral's dress belt, a dispatch case bearing the initials of Flag Officer, West Germany, some German gramophone records of the 1940s – it was, rather to my present regret, abandoned.

Clear light, the trees just starting to turn. Out at sea ships tow filigree wakes over water suggestive of glycerine. The wooded curve of Tallinn Bay protects its islets like an outflung arm. Below Kohtuotsa Vaateplats the conical towers of the Great Coastal Gate and the circular bowl of Fat Margaret's Tower housing the Maritime Museum create a floating vision of Kentish oast houses. From Toompea you can pick out the curiously named guild houses, the Three Sisters and Three Brothers, narrow, yellow fifteenth-century buildings that seem to have been compressed like sardines in a tin. Nearby, at 26 Pikk Street, a similarly yellow building bears the name "House of the Brotherhood of the Blackheads", an organization of unmarried merchants named after their African patron saint, St Mauritius. Further down the same street a grinning face in

stone peering through glasses identified the chemist who was
supposed to have spied on the women opposite, his former
guild house now known as the Peeping Tom building. Some
streets in the old town of Tallinn are so narrow that you could
as easily touch your neighbours as spy on them.
On such a morning the city seems fixed in time, jellified.
Only a distant hydrofoil buzzing south like a gnat lends a
frivolous footnote to its gravity.

I wanted to have a look at the last address Schlemmer wrote
from in Haapsalu, about two hours distant by bus across
flat country over which the road runs to the sea straight as
a ruler. On either side thick woods have narrow paths cut into
them; men on bicycles with dogs at their heels cycle to distant
cottages. From time to time the woods give way to cornfields
or grazing land, the country taking on a peaceful park-like air
remote from ideas of warfare or military trespass.

Estonia's industry is centred mainly on Narva on the north-
east coast, a fortress port slightly nearer to St Petersburg than
to Tallinn. Narva was virtually destroyed when the Russians
retook the city from the Germans in 1944, but since then,
with a largely imported Russian population, it has become the
provider of most of Estonia's energy.

There are few signs of industry on the Haapsalu road,
a spattering of isolated barns in open country or embedded
in forest the only signs of habitation. The bus stopped at
intervals and women in head scarves disembarked and set
off, apparently to nowhere. There were cultivated patches
between woods, where rows of women bent double, pulling
up cabbages and potatoes.

At one of these stops I got out my cigarette case, a cheap tin
affair with a picture of the battleship *Potemkin* and a red flag
with ОКТЯБРЬ printed on it. It had been a present from a
Russian sailor after we had safely landed convoy JW51B with its

planes and tanks in Murmansk. A woman asked for a cigarette and, seeing the Russian flag and word, assumed I must be Russian. We were spared an unpromising conversation by the driver's honking summoning us to our separate seats.

The road was smooth as an egg and the bus roared along merrily. The bus station in Tallinn is on the outskirts of the town, to reach which, you have to cross the grimy Soviet-built suburbs, a world away from the raised quiet of the exotic, medieval centre.

It was not hard to understand why Schlemmer had settled on Haapsalu for his last port of call, nor why he had found Kaplinski's poetry so sympathetic. The forest that encloses the road gives the impression of leading to the end of the world, the light seeming to die among the reeds and lagoons of the sea edge. There appears to be nothing beyond. Kaplinski's poetry, when I began to read it, came to me as an obvious accompaniment to recollection, to tired waters dyed by sunset, ducks and geese pottering about in marshes, memory recapitulating the small details of nature. A lost world recaptured in its infancy.

In the bus I opened Kaplinski's book *The Wandering Border*, whose first poem begins:

> The East–West Border is always wandering,
> sometimes eastward, sometimes west,
> and we do not know exactly where it is just now:
> in Gaugamela, in the Urals, or maybe in ourselves.

Kaplinski, whose Polish father failed to survive deportation to a Russian labour camp, was born and still lives on the opposite, eastern side of Estonia, in Tartu, near Lake Peipsi, the huge lake which forms most of Estonia's border with Russia. "My childhood passed in Tartu," he wrote, "a war-devastated university town. It was a time of repression, fear, hypocrisy and poverty." In another poem Kaplinski wrote:

I could have said: I stepped from the bus.
I stood on the dusty roadside where
a young maple and dog-roses grew.
But really, I leaped into the silence,
and there was no land, no surface to step on.
The silence closed over my head:
I saw how the bus had just departed,
and sinking deeper and deeper
I heard only my own heart beating,
and in the rhythm of it, I saw my own street
passing with all its well-known signs:
lilies-of-the-valley and Equiseti Silvestres,
Oxalis nearly in flower,
an anthill covered by a brownish ripple –
the ants themselves. The Big Pine. The Big Spruce.

In nearly every poem of the three books so far translated
into English there is an appropriation of domestic detail.
He shrinks the world to a few patches of vegetable garden,
a backyard, a nearby wood, a country lane:

This summer is full of insects.
As soon as you go to the garden,
A cloud of flies buzzes around your head.
Bumblebees nest in the birdhouses,
wasps nest in the hazel,
and as I sit at the window
I hear a buzz I cannot name,
whether the voice of bumblebees, wasps,
or electric lines,
a plane in the sky, a car on the road,
or the voice of life itself that wants
to tell you something from the inside out.

The road and the bus journey come to an end at Haapsalu railway station, an elaborate blue-painted wooden structure about the length of Buckingham Palace and with an imposing central clock tower. On either end vast waiting rooms, with floor-to-ceiling windows, resemble art-nouveau conservatories. The station was built in 1905 to receive Tsar Nicholas II, who came to Haapsalu for summer holidays. I had wanted to arrive by rail, train being my favourite method of travel, but the service has been allowed to lapse. The platform, presumably to accommodate the Tsar's entourage, was the longest I have ever seen, and though the lines themselves seemed in order, the sense of dilapidation and neglect was depressing. The Soviets as a matter of policy allowed anything reminiscent of former glories to decay. There were the sporadic noises of hammering and a bit of painting to the wooden columns and portico, but the cosmetic improvements seemed more for the benefit of the bus travellers than for any railway enthusiasts.

The station, at the extremity of the town, is now half-lost in overgrown scrub and wood. I became friendly with a little dog of no certain lineage. He seemed not to belong to anyone but kept rushing on to the platform as if expecting a train. Disillusioned, he would slump down with paws outstretched and the most melancholy of expressions. I had the fancy that he was accustomed to seeing his master off to work in the morning and then greeting him on his return. He knew the time of the trains. Then one evening, at the appointed time, there was a train but no familiar face. A general deportation had taken place, but the dog did not give up, every day at the same time meeting the train. Now there was no train, but habit and hope remained strong.

I watched him follow various workers as they set off home on their bicycles, hoping he belonged to one of them. But one after another they left him in their dust and, after a disbelieving stare, he would turn round and trot back to the station.

Haapsalu, which I had imagined from Schlemmer's account of it, to be on the lines of Bosham or Chichester Water, was at first a disappointment. From the bus stop you enter the town proper by means of a roundabout, leading in one direction to a shopping precinct that could have been in Milton Keynes. There was a new hotel, all glass and chromium, and on the other side of the road the entrance to a graveyard in which the vegetation had run riot.

The long main street began eventually to lose its anonymity, there was a sense of sky lightening at the end of it, a brackish smell of water. The feeling is soon of a country village, with leafy lanes disappearing into open country, and attractive wooden cottages, with ornate verandas, lining the main avenue. You come to the shell of a once imposing structure, the thirteenth-century Haapsalu Episcopal Castle, both cathedral and fortress. The Romano-Gothic cathedral, with its sad memorial to the people deported to Siberia – a box holding Siberian earth and labelled 1949–89 – still functions. But if the castle walls have collapsed at various points, there is enough of them and the bleak cathedral façade remaining to suggest that invaders must have had their work cut out.

The castle stands in grounds now used for football and overlooking them is what is known as the Window of the White Lady. This is supposed to celebrate the grisly story of a castle monk who fell in love with a village girl and disguised her as a boy. When she began to sing in the choir the deception was revealed. The girl was built into the walls and the monk chained up in the cellar. The "White Lady" is reputed to return every August at the time of the full moon and to show herself at this window.

Although Haapsalu has lived under Russians for nearly 300 years, except for the brief between-wars interlude of the Republic, and was recently a Soviet military base, it seemed to

me to have shed its Soviet past completely. The earlier masters
of Haapsalu were the Swedes and the area, with its small
bays, wooden chalets and saunas, has a Scandinavian feel to it.

There is a café in the square between the castle and the
sea. As I ate a rich meaty soup, drank some vodka, I read
Kaplinski.

> This morning was cold, but it warmed about mid-day.
> Blue clouds piled up in the north.
> I came from a meeting – a discussion of
> the teaching of classical languages –
> and I was sitting by the river with a friend
> who wanted to tell me his troubles.
> The water was still high . . .

The café must have been Schlemmer's local and I imagined
him with a German newspaper and a beer, biting off the end
of a small cigar. The smell of stale cigar was often on him. This
was not country sympathetic to Germans, but I presumed
Schlemmer's Estonian links had enabled him to submerge
the more obvious signs of his German officer-class origins.

"We always live our childhood again/Even then, we don't
want it back," Kaplinski writes, but it is hard not to believe that
for someone like Schlemmer, brought up in the headiest
days of the Third Reich, comparisons between childhood
expectations and the present must often have been bitter.

But, as I soon learned, Haapsalu is a restorative place,
known as a cure for the vanities and ambitions of worldly
men. Soviet commanders used to soften and relax in Baltic
mud, their flesh pummelled by imported masseuses, and
before them the Tsars, in the long summer evenings, wound
down at the casino or in walks along the wooded bay.

It is only a matter of a few minutes' stroll from the café to
the beach. The once elegant casino and bandstand, though in

rickety condition, the paint peeling, still exist, and the beach houses, set back from the shore among birch trees, show signs of recent occupation.

You could end your days here peacefully, I thought, a woman and a dog for company, enough money for simple food and a few drinks. But you would have to have exhausted the noisier excitements, the wilder dreams. For someone bruised by history, this silvering sea and silence must have seemed a paradise.

As I explored the inner and outer reaches of the estuary, the wind scissoring the reeds and the water plopping against the sides of jetties, I was reminded of how in Hamburg at the end of the war a Dutch lieutenant and I used to take out a boat and sail it on the Alster. The same silvery light like that of old mirrors, the constant slap of waves on hulls, flotillas of dowager-like geese, swans, ducks taking the water in unruffled serenity. There were a few dinghies here, some beached sailing boats. Schlemmer had been a skilled yachtsman and like Ransome before him must have relished the inlets and litter of islands off Haapsalu Bay. I wasn't sure how much money Schlemmer had left for his old age or if he could have afforded a boat, but the temptations must have been great.

There are reckoned to be over a thousand islands off the coast of Estonia, the two largest, Saaremaa and Huumaa, lying just west of Haapsalu. Largely undeveloped, their reedy shores the mating grounds of swans, these islands have apparently managed to retain a rural innocence despite their attraction as bolt holes for communist dignitaries.

The beaches at Haapsalu suffer from the same degree of pollution as the rest of the Baltic, swimming, it seems, a relic of easier times. There is a beach the locals call African Beach, so named for statues of elephants and lions, but its now forlorn, neglected air reinforces the solitary quiet of a bay largely shielded from open sea. Tchaikovsky used to holiday here, and where he used to watch the sunset there is a bench inscribed with his portrait and a few bars from his 6th Symphony. If I continue to see this remote spa in Schlemmer's terms, it is because the link with him is so long established in my memory. A quality of light, of low suns and green sea, brackets together two dates.

Walking back up the long Posti Street, with its shawl, jersey and craft shops, and past the cemetery to the railway station and its guardian dog, was the beginning of goodbye. Schlemmer perhaps lay here buried under a coat of leaves, not in Tallinn's forest, but the graveyard was gloomy and menacing and the various plots seemed to run into one another, most of them unmarked. After so many deportations, so much killing, the individual death must have come near to a banal anonymity.

The road back to Tallinn, a white parting in a close-curled scalp, took us the whole way into a westering sun. That night I returned to Kaplinski to try and discover what had caused the marked changes in his poetry. The influence of his anthropological interests, his reading of Radin and Lévi-Strauss, his Chinese philosophy and Buddhism, are clear in the ideograms and short, frequently enigmatic poems in his first book *The Same Sea in Us All*. "Painting a boat you need not paint the water." Haiku-like in their gnomic simplicity, his early poems simply *are*, they state, without any desire to amplify:

> Oven
> alone
> in the corner
>
> grandmother
> alone
> in the graveyard

> the same
> big gray
> handmill.

> the wind
> of May
> rolls
> over us

A kind of object-placing suffices in poem after poem. They could be watercolours, only words are obliged by their nature to be specific, even if meanings can remain ambiguous,

> Ink not yet
> dried
> loaf of bread
> not yet
> eaten

> spring
> come
> and gone

These might suggest they are the poems of an old man who has narrowed his horizons, but Kaplinski was barely into his forties when he wrote them.

These earlier poems are narrow on the page, two or three words to a line.

> Honeybees
> through
> sunshine

rising
dancing
falling
dust

Bees figure in several Kaplinski poems, sails, too,
unsurprisingly in a poet whose small country barely separates
the Baltic and the sea-like waters of Lake Peipsi.

Sails come sailing out
from foreign pictures
sails on the Yangtze
sails on the River Li

Sun
golden fish swimming over green rocks
sky with birds
seen through falling petals

Look to the east the shadow
of a white cloud
slants over glittering water
on the horizon
emerging
white sails   sails   sails

Kaplinski's poems in this first book have the purity of
Eluard's poetry, but there are also poems of greater width
and complexity of syntax, poems that combine the rush of
history with romantic, naturalizing imagery. With the flat
landscape and its pockets of forest flowing by outside the bus
window, Kaplinski resurrects the same countryside not only
depopulated but leaned upon.

This emptiness is great indeed,
as is the land. Each one is someone else
from everywhere, and leads the way
somewhere else, and no one could ever
walk through all this land . . .

My abandoned land, lifeless land, how
I try to tear myself away from you, how
can I be and live with all these new things
that have no known face or manner?

The poems in *The Wandering Border* are those of a man who has chosen to keep his eyes fixed on the ground in front of him as his only means of mental sanctuary. Kaplinski did involve himself briefly in politics after the departure of the Russians, but while these poems were being written he was teaching. Poem by poem he builds up a picture of the simple life, domestic activity as a way of survival:

Potatoes are dug, ash trees yellow,
sunflower seeds, ripe apples rotting
under the apple tree – as always,
we have more works than days and something
is always left unharvested, unpicked, unfinished.
The plot has to be dug, the fence needs mending.

And again:

Four-and-a-half tons of Silesian coal –
a whole day to shovel it into the cellar,
a whole winter to burn it. I'm happy to have it,
and – as always – I regret a little
that I must burn something so wonderful.

Kaplinski, with his leanings towards Taoism and Zen, is susceptible to the picturesque but properly sensitive to its limitations.

> Once I got a postcard from the Fiji Islands
> with a picture of sugar cane harvest. Then
>   I realized
> that nothing at all is exotic in itself.
> There is no difference between digging potatoes
>   in our Mutiku garden
> and sugar cane harvesting in Viti Levu.

And he makes an analogy with writing poetry:

> It's the same with poetry – seen from afar
> it's something special, mysterious, festive.
> No, poetry is even less
> special than a sugar cane plantation or
>   potato field.
> Poetry is like sawdust coming from under
>   the saw
> or soft yellowish shavings from a plane.

Kaplinski's latest book *Through the Forest*, though written during the Soviet presence, is the only one to have been published after Estonia became independent. The poems now have long, meandering lines, of a piece with the strolls and forest walks that are their main subject. At the centre of the book, in the title work, the poetry has slipped into a kind of prose poetry. There is a meticulous describing of every aspect of a day-long excursion, from its origin – "Sometimes it is necessary to go. To the forest or the sea or even the shed loft or the old sauna. I go to the forest" – to its ending twenty pages later: "I reach the hill. In front of me I see the

white willows and spruces. Then the slate roof. Here is home.
Here I live. Here we live."

It is a curious poem, almost as if imagination and invention
had given out and been replaced by cataloguing. As if it was
necessary to mark time, to observe and note, no matter how
trivial, to see things on their own terms and not draw conclu-
sions, and at the same time become invisible "as in childhood,
when I crept under the blanket in the big bed and pretended
to be a badger or a fox".

The walk is at snail's pace. "If I see something significant,
then after a moment I stop and write." Dandelions are the first
objects to claim recognition, "waiting for the wind before they
can make their parachute landings", then birch trees, a black-
cock, a Hungarian lilac, a puddle swarming with mosquitoes,
strawberries in flower, a maple.

"I'm really writing a travel book. This time I could not go
to Sweden, so I have come to this forest." But his attempts
to find associations, metaphors, are continually impeded by
the mosquitoes. "No wonder, then, that our people did not
produce speculative philosophers. We had mosquitoes."

It is not a walk of much incident, but the forest scents, the
threat of rain, the sudden noise of pigs rootling, of a cuckoo
singing, come off the page cleanly enough to make one the
writer's companion. We feel the humidity, encounter a cattle
grazing area surrounded by barbed wire. "The barbed wire
has grown into the tree trunks. The trees do not recover from
it, the wound stays forever."

In a clearing there is a solitary columbine, a purple lilac,
a decaying cartwheel, a collapsed cowhouse and threshing
room. Kaplinski writes, "Poetry is like walking somewhere . . .
but you take the actual walk within yourself. If you do. You
set off as one, you come back as another. If you do."

These are not the notes of a botanist observing specimens,
but the dutiful records of a man who has found it necessary

to leave himself for a brief period, to exchange interior life for exterior. "I have paid so little attention to myself, I have lived only outward, toward the forest, the bilberries and pines. Now I am going home, and toward myself."

I began that night to imagine the mosquitoes, or were they actual ones? The biting seemed only too real, but in the morning there were no signs. Instead I was left with the sense of having been on a long, solitary walk, one that led to no flights of fancy or speculation, but which led one into the country's soul. The landscape all round is undramatic, there are no mountains or large rivers, few undulations. But because of its very ordinariness, the birches with their shining, silk-stocking trunks, the occasional rumble of a tractor, impinge on one with greater force. Kaplinski is a poet who keeps close to the ground like a truffle hound, one smells the wet earth on him as he forages for delicious scraps. In his country's new-found freedom he may be tempted further afield.

Back in Tallinn on a Sunday night, the bells of Alexander Nevsky pealing frantically and, inside, the usual throng, roughly dressed, crossing themselves. The prayers and the chanting drift in and out of the incense as if being conducted under anaesthetic. In contrast to the comparative youthfulness and energy of the Lower Town, the girls attractive and fashionably dressed, the worshippers up here are old and poor, their skins the sickly green I associate with post-war Germany. It is a curiosity that my friendship with a German should have, in a sense, led me here to a country lately occupied by the Soviets, and which became his home. Tallinn reminds me of the period in my life when I first knew Schlemmer and many like him. The smell of sour bread and old boots, of flapping mackintoshes and woolly hats. It was the boots of the Wehrmacht that first hounded the Estonians into shadows, and after that the Russians, no improvement at all. Conscripted into the SS, the lowest elements among the dispossessed were sent east to fight and those that survived rounded up to serve the Russians and sent back.

Listening to the bits of German and Russian drifting about up here on Rahukohtu Street, the gulf spread out below, is like listening to mutterings of superannuated boxers, glowering in their respective corners between rounds. The suspicion and bitterness may remain, but the fisticuffs are over. For the present, anyway. It does not take much imagination, however, to people Viru Street and Harju Street, running like cobbled arteries from Raekoja Plats to the port, with lounging soldiery and at every corner or castle-gate bored sentries. Schlemmer, after his years of living high on the hog, had to endure this a second time, an experience we, at least, were spared in England.

Barbarossa was the name Hitler gave to the German invasion of Soviet Russia – "when Barbarossa begins, the world will hold its breath", Hitler announced to his war cabinet on 3 February 1941, four months before he unleashed his armies against his unsuspecting and unprepared allies – and in his account of that campaign, the bloodiest and most prolonged clash of arms in history, Alan Clark wrote, "In Estonia, Latvia and Lithuania, the population lived through the war in a state of dumb resignation, tempered, during its later years, by a fearful apprehension of the revenge the Red Army would exact on its return."

In the initial stages the German 18th Army and 4th Panzer Group advanced from East Prussia almost unopposed, the former through Riga and Piarnu towards Tallinn, the panzers across the Stalin line that curved south from Lake Peipsi to the Dvina. Further east the Luga river, reaching the sea at

Narva, was the only seriously defendable front between
Estonia and Leningrad. It was defended briefly, but the
fearful SS Police Division, the *Totenkopf*, broke through in
the south and soon the Germans were in striking distance
of Leningrad itself.

Clark makes plain that between the purges within the
Soviet military and the treacherous plotting and squabbling
among senior Nazis there was little to choose. The starving
Russian people, their very future at stake, to say nothing of
their lives and property, showed ultimately that they had more
to fight for.

Leningrad, through superhuman efforts and at huge cost,
survived. Hitler, encouraged by the success of his advancing
tanks in the Ukraine and their butchery, allowed a breathing
space to the attackers of Leningrad, now contained and for
the moment irrelevant to the main battle. The Germans
estimated Russian losses at $2\frac{1}{2}$ million men, 22,000 guns,
18,000 tanks, 14,000 aircraft.

Yet the Russians did not lay down their remaining arms and
in September the snows began. The original plan of taking
Moscow by Christmas required reconsideration.

By now the Russians were running out of tanks and
aircraft. The heavily mauled Arctic convoys, routed via Iceland
and Murmansk, carried what material they could, though it is
disconcerting for those of us who sailed in them to learn that
most of the tanks we carried were regarded by the Russians as
obsolete. The Russians remained implacably suspicious of
anything done to help them and few of the supplies brought
to them by sea were ever put to use.

While the war raged on, such crucial events as the Battle
of Stalingrad and later the Warsaw uprising more or less
passed the Estonians by. They had to suffer in silence, the
focus of the war shifting to other areas, merely postponing
their reoccupation. The Germans used the Baltic to train

their U-boat crews, their safety assured by destroyers such
as TS19, to whose command Schlemmer had been appointed
in 1944. A year later he and I would sail the same sea in
a transaction it would have been impossible then for him
to imagine.

By 1945 the Germans were back where they started, their
country in ruins and their armies wiped out. In comparison with the raping and looting Russians they seemed,
superficially at least, a more civilised, if more sinister race.

If Schlemmer had still been alive and not in some Estonian
cemetery, there would have been much human folly for us to
reflect on together, as well as pasts to exchange. The beautiful
light on Tallinn Bay and the few ships working the Gulf of
Finland would have been sources of appreciation as they were
for Arthur Ransone all those years ago. That, as now for
Estonia, was a time of new beginning.

Four Poems

RABBIT BREEDING IN TALLINN

"After servicing the doe,
The buck falls off
With a coughing noise."

The handbook is explanatory.
Now, in the next room
Of this Soviet-style hotel,

There are coughing noises,
Grunts of satisfaction.
At breakfast two stout ladies

Descend for their *schinken*.
Something is radically wrong
With politics and the plumbing.

ALONG VIRU STREET

They come in from the country
To hawk furs and blouses,
Roses in cellophane.

Bulky as prop forwards,
Countenances razored by wind,
They stand still as sentries

Under bullet-pitted walls,
Demure as debutantes
Waiting to curtsey,

They bring whiffs of the farmyard,
Prostrating themselves on the floors
Of churches, doughty believers.

The roses we buy
Bring colour to the cheeks
Of our sour-smelling room.

TCHAIKOVSKY'S BENCH

*Pyotr Ilyitch Tchaikovsky died of cholera,
25 October 1893. On Africa Beach, Haapsalu,
a bench marks the place from which the composer,
on summer visits, used to watch the sunset.*

A kind of lagoon, airless in summer,
Swans desultorily paddling. A sea-green,
    peeling casino,
Gnats flecking salmon-pink sky.

Facing west, inscribed with his likeness,
A few bars of the 6th Symphony,
His bench weathers under pine.

On his last visit, the century
And the season nearing its end,
There was no inkling –

Operas under way, romances
And pick-ups in sweet harness,
Footmen and farm boys.

Water as always conducive
To composing, ideas in spate.
"I have a predilection," he wrote,

"For songs of wistful sadness."
Insidiousness of water, "nil by mouth",
Silver of birches, light ebbing.

HAAPSALU STATION

At Haapsalu, the end of the line.
A red carpet for the Tsar
Summering here in 1909.

The platform wanders into undergrowth,
A saloon extended for their Highnesses,
Assorted dignitaries.

Saracenic in its filigree,
The booking hall echoes
To the hammering of carpenters.

The old track is grassed over,
Peed on by itinerant dogs.
An idiot punctually turns up

For a train that never arrives.
The end of the line,
Of a summer without hootings,

Without pageantry, a gradual
Denuding of ornament, of icons
And incense. A scatter of the faithful,

Old railway employees, filling in time,
Do duty for passengers,
Absent, mourning the sublime.

PART II

Oslo–Bergen

OSLO. STEAMERS GLIDING over to Fredrikstad and the islands smoothly as illuminated swans. Bow waves like crystal shot with a sunset salmon-coloured and electric green. The *Norge* at its berth with its one raked funnel resembling a twenties P. & O. poster, decks for taking turns on and mid-morning bouillon. We walked for ninety minutes over melting snow and slush past the Fiskehalle to where the huge container ships and car ferries squat toad-like over the thawing wharves.

Sirens' melancholy echo, gangways rattling. We return under the bleak walls of Akershus Fort, the fourteenth-century castle suddenly illuminated. This was the German HQ during the occupation, where many members of the Resistance were executed. Imaginary, dying-away cries as in a Munch painting. Curiously persistent sense of doom embalmed in the adjacent Resistance Museum. More congenial the bar at the Grand Hotel, on the wide central boulevard of Karl Johans Gate, a splendid hostelry built in 1874 and a regular watering hole for Ibsen and Munch.

Odd to think that at Fredrikstad, near the Swedish border, until as late as 1845 slavery existed. All these small fortified towns like Halden and Kongsten with their castles and moats, at the mouth of Oslo Fjord, suggest a gloomier past than one usually associates with the country of trolls and Vikings. As the sunset fades a zig-zag pattern of clouds forms against the liquid light, their ends like the outstretched necks of geese.

10.48. The half-empty Bergen train leaves on time, entering at once the first of several hundred tunnels. Scatterings of

snow on the suburbs, the white workers' houses solidly
grouped and superior to such estates in the Soviet-bloc or
indeed west European countries.

The conductor comes round to announce that at
Honefoss, which we reach at 12.30, we have to switch to
buses for the next three hours owing to repairs on the line.
A familiar tale.

At Drammen the fjord is half frozen, one half reflecting
the overlooking pines that line the hills, the other a series of
free loops and squiggles like a Pasmore abstract. Cranes
double themselves in water, ships under repair covered in
snow. Not a breath of wind, and a feeling of being time-locked.
Reading a biography of Lawrence Durrell, the scenes of his
Indian childhood in sight of the Himalayas not incongruous.

After Drammen the snow untrodden and deeper, with
a long line of hills the shape and size of the South Downs, as
I remember them on certain Christmases.

Sawmills and barns now, with drifts of fog spraying off the
snow and deep ravines with the tops of firs like scrubbing
brushes below us.

Water is never far away, slivers and tongues of liquid lead
reflecting the train as we wind on the first leg north before
turning west. After Vikersund the lake balloons out, a few
cottages with boats put away in their gardens.

We drive for three hours through the Hallingdal Valley, a
bridal landscape with water on one side and forest on the
other. Snow on the birches turns them into coral, ostrich
feathers, while the firs stand sentinel in serried rows. Running
down the rock face above the river, frozen waterfalls coagulate
like candle-drips. A few scattered settlements, each with
a new church, ox-blood-coloured houses, each with veranda,
usually on stilts; then the twisting rock-hugging road into Als.

Another train awaits and once aboard we climb immediately into the sky, past a series of high plateaus water-filled

like suspended basins. The occasional hut now, with steep tin roof, is black. This is bear country but no sign of them. Instead, leafless, bristling hills and razor-edged peaks pasting themselves on the train window.

Snow and sky are indistinguishable, merging into each other, boulders under their surplices of powder like half-buried cattle. The walls of iced rock now close in on the track, an icy blueness floating between them.

At Finse the light begins to go, even the dazzle of snow-fields dimming. This is as high as we can climb, and now in the darkness we slip slowly down across the northern prong of Hardanger Fjord. We arrive at Bergen at 18.33, three minutes late, having crossed over Norway's mountain spine from the furthest east to the sea-bordered west.

The Hotel Admiral, a 1906 converted dockside warehouse, looks across the central wedge of Bergen's numerous water-ways to the mountains. Our room is dominated by an engraving of Nelson's "Last Signal at Trafalgar" by Thomas Davidson, and from our balcony ships of every shape and size can be seen rocking gently against their quays. Off the northern quay the white three-masted barque *Staatsrader Lehmkuhl*, known at the time of its turn-of-the-century launching at Bremerhaven as the *Friedrich August*, remains the largest vessel of its kind in the world, its austere elegance putting most modern vessels to shame. Lying alongside her, a naval frigate looks dowdy. While we watch, an awkward-looking and top-heavy survey vessel with orange superstructure glides in. At first glance Bergen, with its row of pastel-coloured wooden and rather wobbly gabled merchants' houses, dating from the fourteenth century and the heyday of the Hanseatic League, seems to have taken the picturesque to new limits.

The air after the day in the train is refreshingly sharp

but it has begun to rain and the snow on the mountains is
moulting. I don't seem to be able to get the complicated
TV to work, despite endless surfing, but just when I am
about to give up, the magic words "Tottenham Hotspur 2,
Sunderland 0", spring out of nowhere, sending me to bed
happy.

I am here mainly in an act of homage to Nordahl Grieg,
who was born in this city, but the only Grieg ever mentioned
in travel books or brochures is the composer Edvard, who
lived here with his Danish soprano wife, Nina, for twenty-two
years. When the couple died, a rock face on the edge of the
fjord was blasted open to provide a tomb. At Troldhaugen, his
white clapboard villa a mile or two along the coast, Grieg's
piano and desk are reverently preserved, and also the small
red troll to which, apparently, he gravely bade good-night
before going to bed. "I am a troll and this is my gala night,"
Louis MacNeice wrote in a poem during the Blitz, the only
mention of a troll I have ever found remotely endearing. The
shops here are full of the hideous creatures.

Ole Bull, quaintly named, to our ears at least, is the other
great cultural icon here, statues and streets recording his
achievements. He was a celebrated violinist, but, of more
relevance, founder of Norway's National Theatre. He gave
Ibsen his first commissions and later took an interest in the
adolescent Grieg.

Sunday. No spirits allowed in bars or restaurants, and only
beer, or wine at a minimum of £25 a bottle. The fish market
gleams in the cold, hard light – prawns, lobster, shrimps,
salmon, every kind of white fish, giving off the purest of sea
smells, of salt liquidizing.

Shops are shut, but not Rasmus Meyers gallery overlooking
the Lille Lungegårdsvann, a large swan-sailed pond, the same
size as the Round Pond in Hyde Park. Meyers, an astute

businessman, sniffed out a lot of bargains early in his career, founding a handsome gallery devoted mainly to Munch and Dahl, the latter an artist I hadn't heard of but who produced an enchanting series of delicate cloud and sea studies. Several fine Munchs, though his swirling, lugubrious paintings rarely please or move me.

Looking across the glittering waters of Vågen at a row of restaurants, we settled for Madam Felle, which sounded like a brothel but turned out to be a sturdy, brasserie-style affair with leather chairs not unlike a London club. Good fish soup and salmon.

During the early hours increasing engine noise, creaking of hawsers, bridge-telegraph ringing, heralded the arrival of huge container ships and car ferries, berthing below the Bergenhus Fort, a grim walled compound with its adjacent Rosenkrantz Tower. Both date from the thirteenth century, and both were nearly destroyed when a Dutch ship blew up off the jetty in 1944.

By dawn all visiting vessels were safely installed, the harbour criss-crossed by scurrying ferries the size of brightly painted bathtubs. Beneath the hotel powerful catamarans set off for Stavanger and other coastal towns north and south, the shipping offices along the quays already busy with clerks working on registers and manifests.

A sparkling, ice-blue day, cloudless and below freezing. In a dusty second-hand bookshop, managed by a solitary, scholarly lady operating in apparent chaos, I learned that there was a statue of Nordahl Grieg outside the National Theatre just up the hill. She produced an old copy of Nordahl Grieg's book of poems *Friheten (Peace)*, published by Gyldendal in Oslo in 1945; the frontispiece was a photograph of Grieg in the uniform of a captain in the Norwegian army. I bore the book away with me and set off as directed to the National Theatre, now playing *My Fair Lady*. A commandingly full-length statue of Grieg gazed over the surrounding greenery, the lank forelock and air of engaging diffidence giving him a look of Christopher Isherwood.

From there I made my way to the Theatre Museum on the university campus at the top of the town. By mistake I finished up in the Maritime Museum, Nansen, Amundsen and Heyerdahl its reigning stars. I looked up the registry of wartime vessels in the Norwegian navy and was glad to see a photograph of the destroyer *Arendal*, a member of the 16th Destroyer Flotilla, in which, as a liaison officer, I made a number of patrols against E-boats in the winter of 1944/5. My interest in both Grieg and Knut Hamsun stemmed from those days, Grieg having been killed in a bombing raid over Berlin two years before. The writer as sacrificial man of action – he was a symbol to me then in the same category as John Cornford, Richard Hillary, Saint-Exupéry, Alun Lewis, Sidney Keyes and Keith Douglas, youthful casualties with, Saint-Exupéry apart, their work scarcely begun.

The Theatre Museum had not much to offer on Grieg, about whose work I then knew little, but the walk on steep, cobbled streets between mountain and shore provided an exciting glimpse of the city's switchback nature, mountains at the end of every street and sea never far below. As the light faded, the layers of white rectangular houses against the wooded hills took on the appearance of ice blocks, the dark bringing with it glowing chandeliers daubing the fjord. The dark treacle of water shimmered as if lit by Chinese lanterns.

Among wartime legends Nordahl Grieg was one of the most interesting, if, because of the language difficulty, the least read. Even so, his death was not unremarked in Britain, for his adventurous pre-war life, his involvement in the issues of the time in Spain and Russia, had made him a star of the Left.

Grieg was born in Bergen in 1901, a descendant of the famous poet-bishop of Bergen, Johan Nordahl Brun. His parents were both teachers, his elder brother subsequently a director of the leading firm of publishers Gyldendal and a board member of the National Theatre. Precocious and handsome, Nordahl had published by the time he was twenty-two a book of poems and a novel, *The Ship Goes On*, as realistic in its details about shipboard life as the novels of Malcolm Lowry or James Hanley. At the age of nineteen Grieg had worked his way to Australia and back as an ordinary seaman, in the autumn after his return taking up a scholarship to Wadham College, Oxford. He continued to write poetry, but from now on most of his energies were devoted to the theatre. The four plays he wrote between 1927 and 1935 were expressionist in technique, owing a lot to Russian models and avant-garde cinema. He served as a war correspondent in China and Spain, and spent some months in Moscow. Whether he was a paid-up member of the Communist Party seems unclear, but temperamentally he was certainly of the Left, his best plays focusing on the exploitation of seamen and workers by wartime profiteers and capitalists.

In his thirties he seems to have been a more radical kind of Rupert Brooke, the patriotic innocence of his poetry contrasting with the analytical Marxism of his prose and plays. He wrote a critical study called *The Young Dead*, in which he discussed Brooke, Sorley and Owen, casualties of the 1914–18 war, and Keats, Shelley and Byron, who also died young, and some of whose work he translated into Norwegian.

With these interests, it was not surprising that Grieg involved himself in anti-fascist activities in England as well as in Norway. His family were comparatively well off, and it was the contrast between his own comfortable circumstances and the conditions in which most people worked that led to the social protest that made him unpopular with his own class.

But in the late thirties, when others who shared his political views were drifting towards pacifism, Grieg became increasingly convinced that fascism and Nazism could only be destroyed by counter-attack. His two best plays, *Our Honour and Our Power*, an anti-war diatribe against profiteering neutrals during the 1914–18 war, and implicitly Norwegian shipowners, and *The Defeat*, a series of short scenes illustrating the collapse of the French Commune in 1871, both deal with classes rather than individuals, treating the contemporary situation in the manner of tabloid newspapers, using symbolist devices and stark music to powerful dramatic effect.

Both these plays, despite their hostility to bourgeois complacency, were successful and Grieg emerged as a playwright of European stature. In 1938 he wrote a novel whose English hero becomes appalled to learn that his anti-war writing has been warmly received by reactionaries sympathetic to Hitler and Mussolini. He realises that his own detestation of totalitarianism and regimentation has to be shelved in favour of the disciplines necessary for organised defence.

His plays read now as more virile expressions of anti-fascism than anything produced elsewhere in Europe. The techniques employed by Brecht and later by Tennessee Williams and Arthur Miller are evident in all Grieg's plays, and the use, as in *The Defeat*, of actual historical characters such as Thiers and Courbet, helped to give his work immediacy and perspective.

With Norway's neutrality swept aside by the 1940 German invasion, Grieg's passionate identification with anti-fascism made him more than ever eager to play some practical part. He joined the Norwegian army in exile, training in Scotland, then moved to Canada where he took part in some unspecified capacity in anti-submarine patrols in the Atlantic and flew as an observer in Norwegian aircraft.

On the old side – he was thirty-nine at the outbreak of war – for more involving activity Grieg took ship to Iceland in 1942, where our paths briefly crossed. In December of that year I was in Seidisfjord, waiting in *Onslow* for the arrival of the convoy we were to escort to Murmansk. Auden and MacNeice's *Letters from Iceland* were no kind of comfort for what lay ahead. Grieg, however, turned up on his way to the tiny, Norwegian-owned Jan Mayen Island, which we passed to port a few days later in a snowstorm. It was uncertain then whether the Germans had bothered to occupy Jan Mayen; it turned out they hadn't, and Grieg was able to land. From this episode Grieg's poem "The Arctic Island" – "It is Norway's land, now it is all we hold" – derives, and also his much longer poem to King Haakon, in which he celebrates the king's decision to resist until no hope was left.

Grieg returned safely from Jan Mayen, but he was obliged to kick his heels for most of 1943, writing, but not fighting. In September he wrote to his friend and future translator G.M. Gathorne-Hardy from Edinburgh, where he had been taken ill. "These three weeks up here have among other things wrecked my hopes about writing my last three poems from this war. I wanted so much to have covered all sides of Norway's war (I have not adequately written about our mercantile navy) and then my plan was to stop writing, hoping for some sort of action during this autumn."

On 2 December he took off on a night flight to Berlin, presumably in some sort of reporting capacity. The plane was shot down, without survivors.

It is not easy to judge the quality of Grieg's war poems, of which about twenty survive in Gathorne-Hardy's translation. In these versions they have a kind of populist, exhortatory ring, somewhere between Longfellow and early Brooke, but they were meant as rallying cries to his oppressed country-men, to whom they were a source of great comfort. Grieg must have been well aware of the best English poetry being written, and of the modern movement in general, so it is unlikely that he would have written in quite so old-fashioned a manner. Long ago I meant to have literal translations made of some of the best poems in his half-dozen volumes and see what could be made of them by starting afresh. My efforts to do this failed, but with the help of a dictionary and concentrating on the subject matter and intention of his poems I made my own versions, which are in no sense translations.

What does come through is Grieg's immense love of country, heightened by his separation from it. Although born in Bergen, it was the far north that captured his imagination and where he felt most at home. But broadcasting his own poems from London, or having them dropped by air or smuggled in, it was to the whole of Norway, its country people especially, that he appealed.

His most affecting poems deal with actual events or people killed in the struggle against Nazism. On 9 April 1940 the Norwegian warships *Eidsvoll* and *Norge* were sunk by the Germans off Narvik, and in his poem commemorating the sinking Grieg ends with the lines:

> Today has the ocean chosen
> To win us our land again,
> Bluejacket lads from *Norge*
> Hardbitten *Eidsvoll* men.

There were poems recording the deaths of the actor Martin Linge, killed in action, General Fleischer, who commanded the Norwegian forces in England, and Grieg's friend Viggo Hansteen, shot by the Germans in 1941. This last, a particularly evocative poem, begins

> When I had written something, often I came to you

and ends

> That summer is gone. The snow peaks in pure
>   white starlight stand;
> You have broken camp and left us.

There are poems to the Swedes, even to the German soldier:

> Who creates a region
> Where men no longer hate
> Is, more than the might of her armies,
> The guardian of Germany's fate.

It is impossible to guess how much the tone and idiom of Grieg's poetry might have altered in changing circumstances. For someone whose play-writing techniques were so adventurous and experimental, the poetry as we have it so far in translation seems, despite its strength of feeling, curiously out of step.

Grieg seems ultimately to have been a little in love with death, as if he had prescience that he might have felt out of sympathy with the politics and causes to which he had given allegiance. A feeling of guilt that he had not fully shared the sufferings of his countrymen in occupied Norway, where the Germans in retreat behaved with merciless savagery, nor been a more active participant as soldier, runs through nearly all his war poems.

Watching the huge container ships tie up in the outer dock at Bergen, reminded me that many of the early incidents of the war took place in these waters. In February 1940 the armed German supply ship *Altmark*, with 300 British sailors on board rescued from merchantmen sunk by the *Graf Spee* in the South Atlantic, was spotted passing Bergen Fjord. She anchored off Josing

Fjord, with protective Norwegian gunboats alongside. The British destroyer *Cossack*, commanded by Captain, later Admiral of the Fleet, Vian, approached and, despite denials by the Norwiegan officers that there were any prisoners aboard, sent a boarding party over. *Altmark* trained her searchlights blindingly on *Cossack*'s bridge, manoeuvring to ram her, but instead herself grounded by the stern. The prisoners were found under locked hatches in the holds and taken to *Cossack*. Six Germans were killed and only one of the boarding party wounded.

Two months later, Norway having been invaded by the Germans in April 1940, Bergen was the site of an even more remarkable event. Just beyond where the schooner *Staatsrad Lehmkuhl* now lay in elegant serenity, the German cruiser *Königsberg* was tied up. Aerial reconnaissance had sighted her and two squadrons of British Skua dive-bombers were dispatched from the Orkneys to attack. Skuas were awkward to handle, particularly sluggish when fully loaded, and they had 300 miles to cover. They reached Bergen just before dawn, exactly on schedule. The *Königsberg* basking innocently at anchor, was taken completely unawares, crew not even at action stations.

The Skuas went into line astern "like a string of beads threading the path of the sun", as Ian Cameron described it in his account of the action. The Germans belatedly took in the gravity of their situation. The cruiser's guns opened up, supported by neighbouring ships and gun emplacements on the hill.

It was too late, for wave after wave of the dive-bombing Skuas hit their target and the adjacent sea. The *Königsberg* was pitched hard against the mole and lifted out of the water like a forward at a rugby line-out. There were direct hits amidships and on a gun turret and she caught fire. The magazine exploded and she rolled over on her side, capsized and sank.

The Skuas flew low over the fjord, euphorically machine-gunning other German vessels in harbour, before zig-zagging out to sea. At Lyso Island they reformed and set off home. One plane was missing. When they reached their Orkney base four hours later they hadn't enough fuel, it was said, to "cover an upended penny".

The two leading pilots of this adventure, Lieutenant Lucy RN and Captain Partridge of the Royal Marines, were not able to enjoy their glory. Lucy was shot down and killed a month later when taking off from *Ark Royal* and Partridge, taking part in the attack on *Scharnhorst* in Trondheim not long after, was badly wounded. He was picked up out of the sea and spent the rest of the war as a POW.

A curious postscript to the Skuas' classic demonstration of dive-bombing techniques was that while the Germans and the Japanese profited from study of the action, the Admiralty soon dispensed with Skuas, and three years went by before dive-bombers in the shape of the nondescript Barracuda were restored.

At almost exactly the same time as the *Königsberg* was being sunk – the first time a major warship had ever been sunk by air attack – the 2nd Destroyer Flotilla had been ordered to Narvik further up the coast. The idea was to prevent the occupation of the port by the Germans, but when the H-class destroyers – *Hunter, Hardy, Hotspur, Hostile* – entered the fjord in line ahead, they found an unhealthily large German presence already established. A whaler and two German destroyers were immediate obstacles and one of the destroyers was sunk straight off by *Hardy*'s torpedoes.

Soon three further German destroyers emerged from a bend in the fjord and battle was joined. *Hardy* and *Hunter* were badly mauled and could not be saved, the survivors from *Hardy* swimming ashore, where they were given sanctuary by a Norwegian woman and her daughter in their cottage. *Hardy*'s captain, Captain B. A. Warburton-Lee, received a posthumous VC.

Three days later, on 13 April, the battleship *Warspite*, with an escort of nine destroyers, entered Narvik fjord, sinking a U-boat and the eight German destroyers still lurking there.

This was not quite the end of Norway's early involvement in the war, for the aircraft-carrier *Glorious*, on her way home inexplicably unescorted in June from helping in the evacuation of troops from Narvik, was intercepted by the battle-cruisers *Scharnhorst* and *Gneisenau*.

The exchange of gunfire lasted an hour and a half, at the end of which, despite the arrival of two destroyers to lay a defensive smoke screen, *Glorious* capsized and sank. Of her ship's company of 1200, 3 officers and 40 men survived. Both destroyers, *Acasta* and *Ardent*, went down. Why *Glorious* left Narvik so precipitously on her own has ever since been the subject of debate.

The most daring of all the adventurous attacks in Norwegian waters concerned the use of midget submarines. These tiny underwater saboteurs, capable of only 6 knots on the surface, 5 when submerged, could dive to 300 feet. Crews consisted of three officers and one engineer petty officer, all necessarily volunteers. Only 50 feet long and extremely light they could carry two tons of explosives. To be effective they had to get close enough to lay their explosives on the seabed below the hulls of their targets. They were known as X-craft and there were six of them.

It was in Altenfjord that the *Tirpitz*, *Scharnhorst* and *Lützow*, the three princes of the German battle fleet, were known to be holed up in the autumn of 1943. The idea was for the X-craft to be taken in tow from their depot ship in Loch Cairnbawn by submarines, who would then detach them at the entrance to the fjord for the short journey onwards.

Two of the craft never reached their rendezvous, being lost with all hands in passage. *Scharnhorst*, it emerged, had left her anchorage. One other midget disappeared completely, her fate unknown. But the two destined for the *Tirpitz* reached their destination.

At 0400 on 22 September X-7 followed the path of a German minesweeper as it swept out through the gap in the anti-submarine nets at the mouth of the adjacent Kafjord. There were numerous anti-torpedo nets to negotiate and various small surface craft milling about. Several times X-7 got caught up in the nets but managed to wriggle free by diving deeper.

When they finally broke surface, *Tirpitz* was a mere thirty yards off. At 0720 X-7 dropped two charges, one under *Tirpitz*'s bridge, the other under the after turrets.

Having got in they couldn't get out, repeatedly passing back and forth under the *Tirpitz* in an effort to find a gap in the nets. An explosion overhead eventually blew them free but by then air was running out, their night periscope was damaged, and they had no option but to surrender. Shortly after X-7's captain was paraded on *Tirpitz*'s quarterdeck charges from X-6 and X-7 exploded, damaging her so badly she was unable to move for six months. The commanders of X-6 and X-7 both received VCs. A year later RAF bombers finished *Tirpitz* off at Tromsø.

I walked up to the National Theatre again to look at Nordahl Grieg's statue. He had led me to this beautiful fjord, steel-blue in cold morning sun, the hills just beginning to rust. It could have been the west of Scotland, serene and sparkling. But I couldn't get out of my head memories of the series of adventures – which with all their hazards and casualties they seemed to be – that had offset those depressing early days of war, when hardly a week went by without news of some terrible calamity. The idea of Norway acquired, for me and others, a kind of magical resonance, an oasis of glamour at a time of months of uneventful escort duty in *Vivien* up and down the North Sea. The German heavy ships, one knew, were less than a day's sailing to the east, out of sight but not out of range.

I made a further inspection of the silent and beautiful *Lehmkuhl,* for it was just off where she lay that in September 1944 the last midget-submarine attack of the war destroyed a floating dock. We received news of these miraculous visitations with both fearfulness and delight. I was by then based at Harwich and on the Norwegian destroyer *Arendal* we would occasionally steer unnecessarily east so its officers could get an imaginary whiff of their screwed-down country. Nordahl Grieg was a name to conjure with in those days and as far as I was concerned it didn't seem to matter at all that I couldn't speak a word of his language. The war continued to throw up heroic and romantic figures and he was one of them.

Long before I joined *Arendal* I had become familiar with the name of Knut Hamsun. My friend Flint, a Leading Signalman on *Vivien,* was the most voracious reader of novels I have ever known. Each time we docked at Rosyth he would make a bee-line for the second-hand bookshops and public library in Edinburgh. He was entirely self-educated and as far as fiction was concerned had natural taste. Writers like Virginia Woolf, E. M. Forster and Ronald Firbank, who I occasionally tried out on him, were not to his liking, his fancy running more to Europeans and Americans. He appreciated action in hard, lean prose: B. Traven, Hemingway and Dos Passos, Silone and Orwell, Aiken and Nathanael West, James Hanley, V. S. Pritchett and Malcolm Lowry. When for so long the war seemed shapeless and infinite, it was from writers who had made something of tough and exacting conditions that we learned to value the experience for its own sake, without questioning its purpose. Life on the lower deck became more acceptable when viewed as material for literature. In those days the officer rituals and conditions of Conrad's skippers seemed remote from us, but a romantic gloss to messdeck fug, to keeping watch on freezing nights, to hanging perilously over the side when painting ship in harbour, was provided by Hanley's greasers and stokers and the wild seamen in Lowry's *Ultramarine*.

More than any other novelist Knut Hamsun was the writer Flint and I were looking for. In his great novel *Hunger*, published in 1890, the hero spends a starving winter in the city (Oslo) trying unsuccessfully to write. After endless rebuffs and failures, constantly on the verge of starvation but with crazy moments of exhilaration when he finds snatches of inspiration or sells something, he wanders down to the harbour. A Russian ship, the *Copégoro*, is about to sail. Hamsun's "I" has never been to sea but offers his services in one of his typically impulsive decisions. The ship is bound for Leeds and Cadiz.

It turns out they could use a young deck-hand. So the thwarted, penniless writer, eager for adventure, whips off his spectacles, which he has several times been reduced to trying to pawn, and persuades the amused captain to take him on.

The novel begins with the sentence, "It all happened at the time when I was wandering about starving in Christiania – that strange city no one escapes from until it has left its mark on him . . ." and it ends, "Once out in the fjord I straightened up, wet with fever and fatigue, looked in toward the shore and said goodbye for now to the city, to Christiania, where the windows shone so brightly in every home."

Not surprisingly, Flint and I, apprentice writers with as yet nothing to show for it and cast without much consultation in the role of sailors, found the predicament of *Hunger*'s hero sympathetic. The fine Gatsby-like ending suggested promise in departure and, though neither Flint nor I conceived our lowly activities in exactly romantic terms, we had a healthy concern for the safety of our own skins. Hamsun's hero is a survivor, though time and again he is saved from total despair and potential suicide only by chance.

Later in the war, in *Arendal*, I found Norwegian officers who did not share our admiration for Hamsun. This was not surprising, for Norway's great novelist, an instinctive enemy of left-wing radicalism, was seduced by the success of his novels in Germany into allowing himself to be used by the Nazis. Determinedly apolitical in all his writings Hamsun, at a time when Norwegians were enduring a ruthless occupation by the Germans, was photographed with Hitler and wrote approvingly of the Nazis. He was by then in his eighties. Flint, a postman in peacetime, was spared knowledge of this betrayal, for soon after leaving *Vivien* he was killed.

Hamsun was born in 1859, and his great decade was the 1890s – *Hunger* in 1890, *Mysteries* in 1892, *Editor Lynge* in 1893, *Pan* in 1894 – a decade in which he also acquired fame as a playwright. He came of prosperous farming stock from central Norway, but when he was a small child the family moved to the north. Although brought up on the farm, leading a solitary life looking after cattle, he was precocious enough to have completed a short novel by the time he was twenty. Like the hero of *Hunger* he failed to find a publisher and spent a similarly destitute winter in Oslo.

He next tried to make a living by physical labour, first working on the road in the Norwegian countryside, and then in America as a lumberjack. Driven home by ill-health he tried again to make a go of it in Oslo but had an even worse time. He set out again for America, signing on this time as a streetcar conductor in Chicago, spending the summer months in the wheat fields of North Dakota, finally cutting hair to earn his fare home. Back in Norway he published his extravagant and polemical *Cultural Life of Modern America*. He had, in the meantime, acquired by bitter experience the

material for *Hunger,* though in this first novel it was only
the Oslo part that he used.

Hunger is remarkable for the modernity of the technique,
the virile economy of the prose. Nothing much happens in
the book, externally: the hero looks for jobs, visits pawnshops,
publishes an occasional article, tries to write a play, befriends
a whore. All the time, except for the odd day here and there
when someone lends him a few kroner or a kindly editor
advances a few days' keep, he is tormented by hunger. He
becomes weak and feverish, hallucinates and fears madness.
He frequently sleeps rough, wrapped in an old blanket,
soaked to the skin on a bench by the harbour. When he
manages to rent a room, it is never more than a week or
so before he is slung out. Yet, as often as desperate, he is
seized by wild euphoria. He is without self-pity, has no blame
for the system.

Lacking companionship, though somewhere he must
have family, he talks to himself, entertaining fanciful notions
of success, or expressing disgust at his ill luck. Chewing
on bread and cheese on a bench in the public garden by
the castle, he can contemplate producing a serious work
in three parts on Philosophical Consciousness. "Naturally
I'd find a moment to break the neck of some of Kant's
sophistries." Unfortunately, just as he is about to get to work,
he discovers he has left his only pencil in the pocket of his
pawned waistcoat.

There is virtually no sex in the book, the hero too weak to
show interest. In the first English translation of *Hunger* the
only two remotely erotic scenes, one where the whore allows
him to look at her breasts, and the other where his cackling
landlord calls him over to look through a keyhole at his wife
opening her legs to a sailor, her paralysed father looking on
helplessly, were omitted by the translator.

These were restored in later translations, all of which, good or bad, suffer in British eyes from Americanisms – "gotten" throughout, "vest" for waistcoat.

Hunger is mockingly funny, not so much in incident, as in the hero's scathing attitude to whatever befalls him, like his night in gaol. His interior monologues are surreal and anarchic, in a manner that has become familiar in plays and novels written a hundred years later.

Although the narrator occasionally resorts to subterfuge and theft, he is god-fearing and not without a sense of humour. His dignity makes him reject well-meant kindnesses and offers of help, which he later regrets. Hamsun frequently switches tenses, a method that not only provides a feeling of immediacy, but allows the past equal footing with the present. Most evocative of all is his naming of every street and square, shop and office, so that walking about Oslo today one can retrace and experience the small events of *Hunger* as if they were still taking place.

Oslo on an autumn evening in 1996, map spread out in anticipation of reliving scenes of *Hunger*. From his attic room the hero sets off for Market Square and its fountains for a drink of water. He looks up at the clock by the Church of Our Saviour. Happy as a bird he turns up Graensen Street, where a cripple's "wiggly movements" irritate him. He follows two women to Cisler's music shop, returning with them up University Street to St Olaf's Place.

These are very short journeys – in fact all activities in *Hunger* can be plotted in an inch or so of a modern street map.

Oslo's main shopping district is Karl Johans Gate, a broad, tree-lined avenue running parallel with the harbour from the main station to the Royal Palace. The *Hunger* man never ventures far from here. He broods in the Royal Gardens, listens to band music drifting down wind from Students

Promenade and applies for a job as book-keeper to a grocer at 31 Grønland Street.

These are easy routes to follow, and nothing seems to have changed. He retraces his steps to Graensen Street, reads the *Afternoon Times* and stops for a quiet doze in Our Saviour's churchyard.

Waiting to learn the fate of his article lodged with a newspaper, he grows feverish with anticipation and to calm himself sets off up Ullevaals Street into the leafy suburb of St Hanshaugen. He comes to a country road, with farm workers lying on their haycarts singing. Where he found himself gazing out on endless fields, however, there is now a traffic-heavy ring road and all visions of rural innocence are abruptly terminated.

He hurries back to the newspaper office only to find that the editor hasn't read his article yet. Relieved that at least it hasn't been dumped, he sets out via Kirke Street and the theatre for a bench by the harbour, perhaps the one we sat on taking in the view on our first night in Oslo.

He has no room to go to. "In front of me, the sea rocked in its heavy drowsiness; ships and fat, broad-nosed barges dug up graves in the lead-coloured surface and glided on, while the smoke rolled out from their funnels like feathery quilts and the sound of pistons penetrated faintly through the heavy moist air."

After a long sleep he makes his way back to the city centre, to Karl Johans Gate. He remembers the name and address of a painter he had once rescued from a brawl in an amusement park and decides to pay him a visit in Tordenskjold Street. The painter has a girl in his studio and refuses admittance.

It is now late and he sets off on the long walk out of the city to the Bogstad Woods beyond Majorstuen. He gathers together some juniper boughs and makes himself a bed for the night.

Next day he wakes up shivering like a dog and vomiting from hunger. He eventually makes for the Oplandske Café where he hopes to cadge a loan from a friend who works in a bank. The friend shows him an empty purse and he pushes on down Torv Street, weeping.

These gentle, unproductive excursions are easy to follow on foot, though less fun if obliged to sleep out night after night. Picked up by a policeman in the early hours, he pretends he's drunk, returning from a club. He's persuaded to go to the police station and register as homeless. After a night in the cells, registering under a false name, he feels ecstatic. He hasn't eaten for three days, cannot recall a single person to turn to. "But what a beautiful day it was, with plenty of sun and light all round me; the sky flowed like a lovely ocean along the Lier mountains."

It is these bewildering changes of mood that prevent *Hunger* from being depressing. Out on the street he laughs to himself at the idea of introducing himself as a Cabinet Minister and ordering a steak, meanwhile munching on a wood chip to stave off hunger pains.

Next stop is the room of a theological student in the Homansbyen area, usually good for a touch. But Pettersen has moved. After a false call to Toldbod Street, he tracks him down to 10 Bernt Anker Street, but on the door there he finds a note: "H. P. Pettersen, stud. theol. – gone home."

Exhausted, he cheers himself up with the idea of a stroll down to the pier. "The ships lay off the piers, the sea was rocking in the sunshine. There was a hustle and bustle every-where – blasting steam whistles, porters with crates on their shoulders, cheerful loading songs from the barges."

I hadn't thought of Flint for years, but now following *Hunger* man's mad flight hither and thither I wished he could have been with me. Books pass from hand to hand, and with them whole new slants on experience, in the most

arbitrary of ways, and here I was, fifty years later, retracing
on the spot a series of incidents that Flint first put into my
head on an afternoon off watch. I can see him laughing in
the sunshine, the faint gurgle of screws and the screech of
gannets off Flamborough Head a routine accompaniment
to our conversations.

By now the areas between the harbour and the station,
and the waterfront road under the walls of Akershus Fort and
the market, have become so familiar one could find one's way
blindfold. Hamsun keeps his hero under tight control, never
letting him wander out of safe territory.

A good week with food and illusions is followed by a
dreadful period when his work is returned to him, his hair
begins to fall out and he develops nervous headaches. When
a stable door slams or a dog starts barking, "I felt as though
pierced to the marrow by cold stabs of pain. I was pretty well
done for."

Several circuits of the Royal Palace take him back into Karl
Johans Gate and the outside of the Grand Hotel, where he
is tortured by the sounds of people eating and drinking.
He remembers a ship called *The Nun* in port, bound for
Archangel, and contemplates joining it.

At a grocery store the assistant mistakenly thinks he has
paid for something and gives him five kroner in change. He
sets off for a café in Stor Street, blushing with guilt, and orders
a steak. After gobbling it down he is violently sick and has to
revive himself with boiled milk. It starts to snow.

He rents a room in *Food and Lodging for Travellers* in Tomte
Street, which I am unable to find on my map. We are soon
back in the favoured area of University Street and St Olaf's
Place where at No. 2 the pretty whore, with whom he occasionally passes the time of day, lives.

She is at home, alone, and surprisingly admits him. He pours
his heart out to her, omitting nothing. Suddenly regretting

her tolerance, she embraces him and shows him the door.

He has still got his room in the Vaterland district but money has run out, his writing is going badly and the landlady, when not preoccupied by sailor lodgers, is pressing.

He is allowed one final night. Next morning he gets up while it is still dark, walks up Kirke Street and by way of the fortress reaches the wharf where the *Copégoro* is tied up. It is a lovely morning and all his troubles evaporate. He finds the play he has been working on, about monks in the Middle Ages, incompatible with the noise of winches, the rattling of chains, the cheerful shouting of dockers. He tears it up.

What happens to him after he signs on is left to the imagination. If he follows Hamsun's own career, he can expect several years of physical hardship, with, if he's lucky, a maturing talent at the end of it. In Hamsun's case, *Hunger* made him famous. He was thirty-one when it came out and not long after he took up with the Norwegian wife of a rich Austrian. They divorced and this time he married an actress, acquiring a farm in the far north. His final resting place was a grand estate near Oslo, where he spent the last thirty-five years of his life, dying in 1952 at the age of ninety-three.

Isaac Bashevis Singer, introducing Robert Bly's 1967 translation of *Hunger*, compares Hamsun's hero to Raskolnikov in *Crime and Punishment*. "Both suffer extreme need. Both are literary neophytes. Both are highly nervous, virtually bordering on madness. Both are spiritual aristocrats." For Singer, "the whole modern school of fiction in the twentieth century stems from Hamsun, just as Russian literature in the nineteenth century came out of Gogol's greatcoat." As Hamsun's disciples, conscious or not, Singer lists Mann and Schnitzler, Wassermann and Zweig, Bunin and Kellerman, not to mention Hemingway and Fitzgerald and a string of Hebrew writers.

Not surprising in the circumstances that German adulation went to Hamsun's head. Ernst Jünger must have read him and, though no Nazi, Jünger would have shared Hamsun's political philosophy. Orwell rather enjoyed similar experiences, knowing they were temporary and could be used for literary purposes. Hamsun ranted against adversity, but was stoical and self-sufficient. A curious kind of religious belief sustained him and there is no sense that he meant to exploit his suffering.

If the officers in *Arendal* had no great love of Hamsun, it was not only because of his senile support for the Nazis. The experiences described in *Hunger*, and Hamsun's attitude to them, were completely remote from those of an officer class. Hamsun was less concerned in exposing capitalist greed and corruption than, for example, Nordahl Grieg, but he shows no faith in a redeeming bourgeoisie.

Hunger is a great and meticulous evocation of life in the poor districts of a city, as exact in its fashion as Joyce's Dublin or Svevo's Trieste. My old friend William Sansom, describing Oslo in the 1950s, called it a "truly countrified city set on water among virgin hills".

Oslo has sixty miles of fjord, scattered with islands, before open sea is reached. In *Hunger*, because it is a winter book, the sea, "mother of pearl blue" as Hamsun describes it, only comes into effect as escape, but on a good day, in summer weather, the feeling must be of adventure and the expectation of pleasure. Now, in autumn, the city has a soothing, graceful *fin de siècle* air, its cafés and restaurants exuding mellow light and thoughtful bustle. It is grand in the way a capital should be, but on a small scale. At street level it is always easy on the eye.

Four Poems

OFF TRONDHEIM IN *ARENDAL*, 1944

One of those mornings
The sea cleaned flat
As if with a palette knife.

On the horizon carbon smudges,
Slight swell like an exercise book
Scribbled on by ships.

On board, her officers imagine
A coastline invisible to foreigners,
A discoloration of sea

Suggestive of land.
On the breeze they hear
Rustle of birches, running water.

SNOW

Entwined like seahorses
We dream the history
Of the fjord; saboteurs,
Ski-troops, limpet-mines,
Bears making a show
Of solidarity, quislings.

Snow makes us light-headed,
Snipers with eyes of monkfish
Cuddle confiscated breviaries.
Eyelids protect us from sun,
Your body a sanctuary.
Outside, real snow has begun.

RUSSIAN ENGINEER, VIANGA

So faint the scent
She gave off, it seemed breathed
From the lining of her jacket,

Musk emptied of itself,
Mere irritation of air.

Gold epaulettes, ankle-length coat
That swung like a dancer's,
Fur hat with ear-flaps,

In the wreckage of our foc'sle
She was a spectral presence,
Stokers open-mouthed

As though seeing things.
Swatch of blonde hair
Brushing her collar,

A voice like iced smoke,
It was as if we had drowned,
Suddenly come up for air.

BERGEN

A city of statues covered
In birdshit, a leprosy
Of snow. Gangrene setting in.

A switchback
Of a port, easier on legs
Of uneven length.

In Torgalmenningen
A clutter of memorials –
Resistance leaders, soldiers
In helmets like tortoises,
Sea-booted sailors.

A fishy music
In the air, infectious.

Streets show black
As keyboards, a thaw
On the way.

Incised by the prows
Of ships, the inlet
Turns skate-rink,
Clanks like cutlery.

The fjord exhales,
Breathing smoke.

There is a taste
On the tongue
Like wafers, a half-listening.

Five Versions of Nordahl Grieg

THESE POEMS ARE in no sense translations. I have used the subject matter of five of Grieg's poems to write new poems that have little more than a family resemblance to the originals.

SUMATRA GIRL

Heat, unforgettable heat. As also your flawless skin
Grey with malnourishment, your salt-grey skin
And gold-eyed glance, your unmarked nakedness.

Ashore a few hours, then on board
For the Last Dog, tall palms in my eyes,
The sweating jungle, your skin's ivory,
All the way back to Padang.

LINES ON THE DEATH IN EXILE OF GENERAL FLEISCHER, NORWEGIAN GENERAL

Scattered, one-legged companions,
Survivors of Narvik in bleak snowstorm
When rifles red as wolves' eyes
Spat flame at them.

Mimicking animals in their furs
And as defenceless – soldier ghosts in exile
May weep for their commander,
Distant, but like them buried in snow.

JAN MAYEN

Norway of boulder and ice,
Of pine forest and birch,
This our last dependency,
The last land we hold.

Norway of Wergeland and Linge,
Of Hansteen and Ibsen,
Under Arctic snow
We remember what was –

Fjords smothered in blossom,
Lakes in summer mist.
We sail in our mind's eye,
Recoup what is lost.

Arctic island, weatherbeaten rock
Convoys take bearings from.
Your flags flutter resistance,
Red of Norway, blue of blizzard.

EIDSVOLL AND *NORGE*

Outgunned, hemmed in, a slow spring
Meeting the ice-floes, *Eidsvoll*
And *Norge* for the last time
Leave harbour, mountains behind them.

Eidsvoll, where our country was shaped,
Given laws and identity,
Norge, our sacred name,
On the bows of a warship,

Swinging south-west from Narvik,
Chain-saw of peaks in the distance.
Lofoten and Harstad, a scatter
Of islands at the mercy
Of the elements.

Eidsvoll and *Norge,* patrolling
Westward, Stamsund to starboard,
And off the port bow Sørland,
Innocent of any enemy,

They knew of minefields
Laid by the Allies, but not
Of blockade runners, of *Lützow*
And *Blücher, Karlsruhe,*
Königsberg, secretly at sea.

They perished guns blazing,
Sailors from Tromsø and Hammerfest,
Grimstad, Namsos and Molde,
Summer in their eyes.
Long-legged, ice-blonde women

At peace now among seabirds,
Off rocks lashed by the Arctic,
They whisper of retaliation,
Dream new warships
Heirs of *Eidsvoll* and *Norge.*

THE ASSASSINATION OF
VIGGO HANSTEEN

September, and twilight,
What was left of it.
Colour of made-up eyelids,
Hiss of running water.

Guests expected, bottles arrayed
Like soldiers, music down low
A woman, facing the mirror,
Adjusting her silhouette.

A knock on the door.
"You go," she calls to her husband,
Stroking their dog by the fire.
He takes his glass with him.

They are not guests, though,
This time, but two soldiers,
Pistols at their belts,
Feldwebels, uneasy of eye.

They waste no time
On preliminaries, ask
No questions. Their shots
Echo down the fjord.

PART III

Operation Chariot

for Charles Sprawson

SHOULD THE *TIRPITZ*, at last operational, break out into
the Atlantic, only the great Normandie lock at St Nazaire was
large enough to receive her. "Operation Chariot", an assault
by sea, was devised to destroy it. On 26 March 1942, an
ageing, expendable, Lend-Lease destroyer, the *Campbelltown,*
with an escort of the destroyers *Atherstone* and *Tyndale,* and in
company with an assortment of motor-torpedo boats, motor
launches, and one motor gun boat, sailed from Falmouth.
The intention was that *Campbelltown,* loaded with explosives,
should penetrate the German defences on the Loire estuary
and ram the lock gates, blowing them and herself up.

> A mild afternoon, spring nervous
> Among palm trees, advancing
> And retreating. Unremarkable weather,
> Skies clearer than welcome. A huddle
> Of ships that might be trawlers,
> Fishing boats. Looming over them
> *Campbelltown,* two funnels removed
> And slanted in the German fashion,
> Uneasy in disguise. Lightened aft
> To skim over sandbanks, but tricky
> To handle. A dowager in finery.
>
> Falmouth had been a last
> Run ashore, scones, ale,
> Cornish pasties. Back on board

Her bemused crew watched
Finishing touches put to camouflage,
Flags stored with swastika and emblems.

On board *Campbelltown* commandos,
Faces blackened, suffered in slight swell,
The Atlantic building up
On the beam, washing the Scillies.
By nightfall, steering due south
On their 400-mile passage,
They were free of all traffic,
Scurrying cloud mapping the moon,
Silvering bow-waves.

Throb and shudder of engines,
Adjustments to speed, to course.
"Steer 170°." "Up 10 revolutions."
"Midships." Ghostly repetition
Of orders, muffled acknowledgment.

Off Ushant, swastikas exchanged
For the white ensign. Looming to starboard
A scatter of trawlers.
Accordion music and garlic
Drifting from fishing boats.

At first light, the sighting
Of a U-boat, depth-charged
By *Atherstone*. Like a whale
She rolls over, dives deeper.

Hours later, the sea empty,
She surfaces, transmits presence
Of enemy forces. *Campbelltown,*

As a diversionary measure,
Feints to move westward.

Five Möwe-class torpedo-boats,
Alerted, streak from their lair
In St Nazaire, a time-wasting sweep
Past Belle Ile, wrong-footed.

Clouds mercifully thickening,
Cocoa and rum for the run-in,
And that first sense of land,
A lightening of water.
Scent on the wind.

A compromise of ocean.
"Port 10" and then,
Swinging sharply north-east,
A row of lights ahead,
Like a stopped train. Destroyers
Peel off, vanish into darkness.

The tide running high,
So entering the estuary
Was like gliding
Over a sprung ballroom.
MLs, MTBs swoosh
And cavort in *Campbelltown*'s wake,

On possibly their last night
On earth, 62 naval officers,
291 ratings, 268 soldiers,
Muffled in silence,
Hold their breath.

Time at a standstill.
Bow-waves like lip-salve,
All that is visible
As they edge closer,
Screws slithering.

Two miles to go, and now searchlights,
Fingering the darkness,
Pick out each vessel
As if in a circus tent,
Campbelltown, MTBs, MLs.

Morse and Aldis lamps
Stutter out challenges,
And in *Campbelltown*
Leading Signalman Pike,
Specially assigned-German speaker,
Returns challenges in German.
False identification signals, call-signs,
                    implying,
"Friendly forces returning from patrol,"
Stutter from the mast head.

Precious minutes are saved,
The signals interpreted.
Then, suddenly, the whole sky
Splattered with tracer,
Peppermint-green, rosebud-pink,
Like a cabaret. No need now
For dissembling, on *Campbelltown*
Instructions ringing from the bridge,
"Full Speed Ahead, Both Engines."

And now, Mindin Bank to starboard.
They skirt the deepest channel,
Come in range of heavy artillery.
Shore batteries, uncertain still
Of identity, hold their fire,
And *Campbelltown*, making 19 knots,
Attendants in place, skims Grande Rade.

Now, if ever, for blessing.
The navigator on ML310,
Chosen for knowledge of the estuary,
Boozy old peacetime yachtsman,
Remembers *La Frégate* and *Havana*,
Hospitable estaminets, their girls
In black stockings and suspenders,
Little else, one with hole
At the heel, bared like an apple.

Remembers, too, a forsaken 14-footer,
The swirl of water between sandbanks,
A blonde arm sharing the tiller.
He knows the way in,
And *Campbelltown*, following,
Surges at the lock gates,
Lit up as if for surgery.

Abreast, a guard ship,
Buddha-like at the entrance,
Now silenced by pom-poms.
Confused, panicking shore batteries
Rake her, crew diving
Into black water. Scuttled,
She sizzles, subsides.

On *Campbelltown* they hoist
The white ensign, swastikas
Consigned to the gannets.
Now gunfire on all sides,
A party grown raucous,
Campbelltown responding with 4.7s,
Oerlikons, Lewis guns.
Commandos, readying for exit, crouch
Frog-like behind gun turrets,
The quay sliding towards them.

At 01.34, on March 28,
Four minutes adrift on the ETA,
Campbelltown, her crew steadying
    themselves
For impact, cut through torpedo nets,
Rammed the lock caisson. Stuck.

For most, a one-way journey,
Though – what seemed a lifetime ago
Among Falmouth's palm trees
And friendly headlands – plans
Had been laid for withdrawal.
Plans only, not cynically made,
Just provisional, reliant on God's grace.

MLs, cutting across shot silk
Of Penhouet Basin, the bows
Of *Campbelltown* embedded,
Land soldiers under stage lighting,
Crews reduced to ants.
Gunboats, like clockwork toys
Gone demented, circle in patches
Of burned oil, the Old Mole

Like a basin blood-filled
After an attempted suicide.

On shore, buildings go off
Like fireworks, demolition parties
From *Campbelltown* laying waste,
Startled sentries up-ended
By rugby tackles. Men stagger
Along quays like drunks
Or headless chickens, bleeding.

The commandos, cut off,
Nowhere to go, roamed
Into captivity or oblivion.
They never had a price,
Token counters in a board game
Invented by others.

Campbelltown, meanwhile, nursed
    wounds,
Bombs foetal in her hold,
Crew captured or hiding. Like a dog
Wanting to be put down
She lay on her side, mute.

Next day, at noon,
Decks thick with German officers
Inspecting their booty,
Imaging the exercise over,
She blew up, taking them with her.

An expendable ship, chosen
For her expendability, but reliable,
With her last breath wiping

The smile off the face
Of her visitors, a delayed welcome
Removing the cream of them.

She went down unattended,
Alone, what remained
Of her crew too distracted
For the tears that she merited.
Around her lay fragments
Of gunboats, bodies floating
On wreaths of refuse.

Sailors have no recycling,
Calculated sacrifices
For whom trumpets may sound
Across oceans, but whose
Simple ambitions, pleasures
In drink and swearing,
Sink with them. Not for them
The luxury of post-mortem.

As a result of the attack on St Nazaire the Normandie dock
was rendered useless for the rest of the war. U-boat headquarters and all German naval operational centres were
shifted inland in fear of an Allied landing.

In Operation Chariot the Royal Navy lost 85 men, the army
59, out of a total force of 630. The 106 sailors and soldiers
taken prisoner included Lieutenant-Commander S. H. Beattie,
captain of *Campbelltown*, who received the VC. German losses,
as a result of the explosion in *Campbelltown*, and the repeated
torpedoing of the lock gates by MTB74, were reckoned to
be higher.

Today the neglected naval port of St Nazaire, on either
side of the flat banks of the Loire estuary, bears no record of

these events. They are old history. The cafés and restaurants remain, but there are few sailors. My own interest derives from the same year as Operation Chariot, since my first ship, the V. and W. class destroyer *Vivien*, was commanded, before his posting to *Campbelltown*, by Lieutenant-Commander Beattie.

PART IV

Buxtehude

PASTED INTO MY copy of Ernst Jünger's *Gärten und Strassen*, a journal running from 3 April 1939 to 24 July 1940, is a piece of paper on which is stamped *Admiral der Nordsee, Buxtehude*. On the flyleaf I had written, "S/Lieut. Alan Ross, RNVR, Wilhelmshaven, June 1945." Between Jünger's opening diary date and my acquisition of it, the most appalling war in history had come and gone. Jünger, the most decorated soldier of the 1914–18 war and one of the few writers of stature to have remained in Germany, somehow managed to take part in the 1939–45 war yet stand outside it. It was, as I gradually learned, a trick he had come to perfect.

I can't remember now whether the page from the Admiral's jotting pad was already in the book, or whether I stuck it in later. If I acquired it in Wilhelmshaven in June 1945, then it was before the staff of the Flag Officer, Western Germany, to which I was attached, moved in August the hundred miles or so inland to Buxtehude. This had been a few months earlier the headquarters of the German North Sea fleet.

The book, bound in field-grey linen with the title in an appropriate grass-green, was published by E. S. Mittler and Sohn, Berlin SW68. At the back, on pages now grown apricot-coloured with age, were listed other works by Jünger, the legendary *In Stahlgewittern*, his account of front-line experiences during the First World War, published in 1920, *Der Kampf als inneres Erlebnis* (1922), *Das Abenteuerliche Herz* (1929), *Der Arbeiter* (1932), *Afrikanische Spiele* (1936), and, unexpectedly, *Auf den Marmorklippen* (1939), a novel whose ambiguously written but undeniably hostile attitude to totalitarianism, war and developments in Germany, led many important Party officials to call for Jünger's arrest and the destruction of his book. Luckily for Jünger, his fame as a hero of 1914 and as a writer who elevated soldiering into something both chivalrous and spiritual, saved his bacon. Hitler ordered that he was not to be touched. Others, less critical of Nazi activities, were not so fortunate.

At that period, due to spend the next eighteen months in Germany and speaking German a good deal better than I do now, I had time on my hands. I acquired most of Jünger's books and, attracted by the stony elegance of his prose, as simple to read in its way as Simenon's French, I worked my way through them during a summer and winter in the flat farmlands of Ostfriesland and the Elbe valley.

Jünger began to interest me as an heroic figure at a time when heroism was suddenly at a discount. Despite his appalling experiences as a storm trooper in the 1914 war and his unease, only obliquely expressed, with Nazism, his military pride and fierce patriotism led to a renewal of his belief in the glory of war. Although it seemed a perverse idea in the context of Germany's mutilated soldiers, starving citizens and flattened cities, it was not only people like Jünger who found in his involvement with machines and death an extra dimension.

He was, essentially, an aesthete rather than a convincing polemicist and he was able to devise techniques, most especially elaborated in *Auf den Marmorklippen* (On the Marble Cliffs), for squaring conscience with behaviour.

The mood of this short novel, 120 pages divided up into thirty sections, is wistfully reflective. Its opening words – "You all know the wild grief that besets us when we look back on times of happiness. How far beyond recall they are" – set the tone, continuing, "Sweeter still becomes the memory of our years by moon and sun when their end has been in the abyss of fear . . . So it is that I think back to the times when we lived on the Great Marina – it is memory alone that evokes their charm. In those times, I will confess, it seemed to me that many cares and many troubles darkened our days, and, above all, we were on our guard against the Chief Ranger."

Jünger began and finished his novel in the six months before the outbreak of war. In its study of tyranny, as exemplified by the Chief Ranger and his marauding gangs who threaten the community living in the shadow of the Marble Cliffs, it is necessarily vague in characterisation but not in theme. The imaginary landscape, with its forest, lakes, rare plants and vipers, derives from Jünger's visits to South America, Italy, the Bodensee, and while the feel of the book is northern the climate is often romantically southern. The alternating periods in which the events take place are never identified.

Reading it so soon after Germany's defeat was inevitably to see it as an allegory of Nazism, but despite Jünger's claim for it to be a study of the nature of tyranny in general and of any totalitarian state, it seems just as specific now. The curiosity is that, despite the disguise of anachronistic weapons and weird costumes given to the criminal elements engaged in their subversive activities, Jünger's book was able to be published on the eve of the Second World War and to sell in large quantities.

The plot, such as it is, has few ramifications. The narrator and Brother Otho, former soldiers who are now part of a secret Order, live in seclusion in a hermitage on a rocky outcrop on the edge of the Marble Cliffs. They are botanists, collectors of rare plants, enjoying rather than fearing the company of the lance-head vipers that cover the surrounding paths with their "hieroglyphics like a papyrus roll".

The Brothers' studious, dedicated way of life is upset by reports of acts of violence committed by robber bands under the auspices of the Chief Ranger, a man of vast power, wealth and appetites. Feared by everyone, he operates by threat and rumour.

The Brothers, in face of these, enter a period of decline: "From hollow joy we sink to leaden sorrow, and past and future acquire a new charm from our sense of loss. So we wander aimlessly in the irretrievable past or in distant Utopias; but the fleeting moment we cannot grasp."

The Brothers are themselves not immune to the lure of power, though of a different sort to that exercised by the Chief Ranger, "for is that not the eternal pendulum that drives on the hand of time by day or night?"

Bit by bit their quality of life by the Marina begins to alter. "It was the old life, and yet something had changed in it. Sometimes when we stood on the terrace and looked out on the encircling gardens we seemed to catch a breath of hidden listlessness and anarchy. It was then that the beauty of the land touched our hearts with pain."

A cloud of fear "like a mountain mist that presages the storm" precedes the Chief Ranger, whose power seems to dwell in the threat enveloping him rather than in his own person. On occasions the Brothers climb to the top of the Marble Cliffs to look down on the territory under the Chief Ranger's domination. "Far below lay the Marina, edged with little towns with walls and watch towers dating from Roman times; high above them rose age-grey cathedrals and Merovingian castles."

In this confusing, ambitious countryside, with its vines and fruits, the Brothers become increasingly aware of its frontiers, "the mountains where lofty freedom but not plenty found its home among the barbarian peoples, and towards the north the swamps and dark recesses where bloody tyranny lurked."

Feuds had always been a part of life in the countryside, the farmers and herdsmen quarrelling over cattle and land, but now a web of secrecy develops. Spies infiltrate the forest and crime increases. "In this way the old forms lost their sense." Bands of marauders attack people at night, breaking in and torturing them. "Far more menacing still was the fact that all those crimes which set the land in an uproar and cried for justice, went almost entirely unavenged. It even came to such a pass that nobody dared any longer speak of them openly."

There are good days in the Marina nevertheless. "Herein, above all, lay a masterly trait of the Chief Ranger. He administered fear in small doses which he gradually increased . . . like an evil doctor who first encourages the disease so that he may practise on the sufferer the surgery he has in mind."

Foresters, huntsmen and gangs of mercenaries roam the country, entering the forests into which gipsies, heretics, fugitives, magicians and witch doctors have taken refuge. The Chief Ranger from time to time has "a dozen or two strung up like scarecrows on the trees if they seemed to spawn too abundantly." His own henchmen, who carry out these tasks, are dressed in green livery, or red coats with black pumps, and are served by naked odalisques who play billiards while the company dine.

There are no references to contemporary life. The Brothers are disciples of the eighteenth-century naturalist Linnaeus, their minds tuned to the study of obsolescent species; feuds in the forest are fought with sword and spears; pagan deities and Christian monks exist side by side. Jünger's language varies from the archaically formal to the pedantically foreign, the exotic descriptive passages like luxuriant overgrowth over stone walls.

Father Lampros, a monk from the Cloister of Maria Lunaris, becomes increasingly associated with the Brothers. Presently engaged in the study of plant formation – "how crystallisation gives meaning to growth as the clock face does to the moving finger" – it turns out that under a pseudonym he is the author of a famous work on the symmetry of fruits.

Father Lampros's "silences were more effective than his words". Of noble family he is both modest and proud, avoiding all scientific wrangles and argument, the embodiment of a Jünger hero. While aware of the dangers threatening the Marina, his monastic life remains undisturbed. "Rather it appeared that his spirits rose and brightened with every step which brought the danger nearer." He takes no precautions for his own safety but under the guise of directing the Brothers to a rare plant warns them of a need to be elsewhere.

While skirmishes multiply below the Marble Cliffs, work in the herbarium flourishes. Tempted at moments to lend their support to one or other of the feuding groups "and to string up the torn bodies of each one that fell into our net at the crossroads", the potentially bloodthirsty Brothers settle for spiritual resistance. "Thus a strange period began for us by the Marina. While evil flourished like mushroom spawn in rotten wood, we plunged deeper into the mystery of flowers, and their chalices seemed larger and more brilliant than before. But, above all, we continued our study of language, for in the word we recognised the gleaming magic blade before which tyrants pale. There is a trinity of word, liberty and spirit."

The Brothers veer between exaltation and depression, joy at the beauty of the landscape, dejection during days when they wander aimlessly about in the herbarium and library. Though they have amassed many volumes of notes about their researches, they have published little. "We were living in times during which the author is condemned to solitude."

The days of low spirits coincide with days of mist, when the Marble Cliffs are lost under white vapour. The sense of danger increases on their expeditions, but flowers directed them "like a compass piloting through unknown seas". Then, one morning, they set out in search of a red woodland orchid, named *rubra* by Linnaeus, only to be found growing alone in thickets or woods. The most likely spot, they guess, is an old clearing called Köppels-Bleek.

Eventually they come upon a specimen, but as they move to examine it they glimpse a further clearing with a barn half-submerged in undergrowth. "Over the dark door on the gable end a skull was nailed fast, showing its teeth and seeming to invite entry with its grin. Like a jewel in its chain, it was the central link of a narrow gable frieze which appeared to be formed of brown spiders. Suddenly we guessed that it was fashioned of human hands fastened to the wall."

The surrounding trees are found to be littered with death's heads. "Many a one with eye sockets already moss-grown seemed to scan us with a dark smile." A dwarf attends this horrifying spot, from which the Brothers flee in disgust, at last apprised of the reality of their fears. "Such are the dungeons above which rise the proud castles of the tyrants . . . they are terrible noisome pits in which a God-forsaken crew revels to all eternity in the degradation of human dignity and human freedom. In such times the muses are silent, and truth begins to flicker like a torch in a current of foul air." Despite their terror the Brothers' conscientiousness demands that they return to the spot to make a note of the red orchid in their field-book.

Some time later a powerful car, "humming softly like an almost imperceptibly vibrating insect", pulls up at the hermitage. Two men step out: Prince Sunmyra, "a noble lord of New Burgundian stock", and Braquemart, "a small, dark, haggard fellow whom we found somewhat coarse-grained". Braquemart hungers after power and mastery but is led astray by his wild dreams into the realm of Utopias. "Like every crude theoretician he lived on the science of the moment . . . he belonged to the race of men who dream concretely – a very dangerous breed."

The young Prince has "an air of suffering" in contrast to

his age. "I had the impression that great age and extreme youth had met in his person – the age of his race and the youth of his body. Thus his whole being bore the deep stamp of decadence; one could see two forces at work in him – that of hereditary greatness and the contrary influence which the soil exerts upon all heredity. For heredity is dead men's riches."

It had been the narrator's hope, as it was Jünger's, that the nobility would eventually leave their estates to be the chivalrous leaders in the fight for freedom. "Instead of which I saw this man old before his time, himself in need of support; the sight made it abundantly clear to me how far decay had gone."

The visit of this strangely paired couple has been occasioned by their concern about developments in the forest. Braquemart, though having much in common with the Chief Ranger, is of a mind to confront him, and with the Brothers establish a new theology, a new order. The Brothers remain hesitant, fearful that "like an unskilled doctor" he will worsen the situation.

Braquemart and the Prince set off on a reconnaissance with nothing decided. "They went like half-men – on the one hand Braquemart, the pure technician of power who saw only fragments and never the root of things; and on the other hand Prince Sunmyra, the noble spirit, who knew the nature of justice and order, but was like a child venturing into forests where the wolves are howling."

Receiving a message from Father Lampros to look after the Prince the narrator follows them, joined by an old herdsman, who picks up a few retainers on the way. They clothe themselves in leather doublets and hoods, seizing halberds, spiked maces, pikes and "all manner of barbed hooks". Two packs of ferocious hounds accompany them.

In the marshes where the Chief Ranger keeps his hides for shooting duck they come upon a noisy rabble. Although much superior in number the rabble, frightened by the dogs, take to their heels. When the dogs are let loose they leap upon the retreating men, tear at their throats, and scatter their bones, "a scene from hell devoid of mercy".

At Köppels-Bleek the Chief Ranger's savage mastiffs are encountered, the leader of them the notorious bloodhound Chiffon Rouge. In the pitched battle that follows, the Chief Ranger's dogs armed with necklaces of blades, there is a moment when the Chief Ranger's loud laughter is heard. It is the nearest that he gets to the action in the whole book.

In the confusion of events the narrator stumbles on the red orchid. But when he looks back at the barn in Köppels-Bleek, he sees that the whole area is on fire and that to the frieze of skulls have been added those of the Prince and Braquemart. Dead and disembowelled dogs circle the corpse of the old herdsman.

The narrator has a sense of being outside of time. "I fell into a half-dream in which I forgot the nearness of danger. In such a state we pass like sleep-walkers through perils, not picking our way, but close to the spirit of things."

He pulls the Prince's head from its pike and bears it away with him. Fires are raging in the forest, looters wander around brandishing torches, others are drunk and insensible. When he reaches the comparative sanctuary of the Marble Cliffs he looks down on nothing but ruin. Villages, farms, cloisters and castles are all burning. "Of all the terrors of destruction only the shimmering golden light of the flames rose up to the Marble Cliffs. So distant worlds flare up to delight our eyes in the beauty of their ruin."

He hears the baying of Chiffon Rouge and his pack as they reach the foot of the cliffs. Still in a dream-like trance he manages to stir himself at the last minute and reach Brother Otho in the hermitage garden.

The hounds break in and are about to spring when the

lance-head vipers slide from their crevices and, rising to their full height, form a circle round Chiffon Rouge and his handlers. "In this posture they swayed their heads, like slow-beating pendulums, and their fangs, bared for the attack, had a deadly gleam like lancets of curved glass. Accompanying this dance, a gentle hissing like iron cooling in water pierced the air, and from the lily beds a fine clatter of horn arose like the castanets of Moorish dancers."

The vipers advance on the men and dogs, coiling round them so they seem to be enveloped "by a single scaly body".

In the library of the herbarium books and manuscripts are in perfect order. A joyous meeting takes place between the Brothers. They wash the Prince's head in wine, laying it in one of the great scent amphorae "in which there withered the petals of white lilies and roses of Shiraz".

Then, together, they leave the house "which had become a warm shelter for our spiritual life and brotherly companion-ship". They make for the harbour, joining bands of fleeing people. Turning to look back at their old home, they watch it go up in flames, together with the Cloister and the solitary figure of Father Lampros. They find space on a brigantine anchored in the bay and set sail. Reaching a mountainous shore, they are welcomed and offered a farm in the shelter of an oak grove. "We passed through the wide open door as if into the haven of our father's house."

Auf den Marmorklippen is a blood-curdling, Wagnerian story, redeemed ultimately from the wilder excesses of melodrama by the beauty of the writing. In few of his books does Jünger show any gifts of characterisation nor interest in conventional narrative, but his visionary power and ability to create indelible images sustain involvement. *Auf den Marmorklippen* contains passage after passage in which the natural world is brought into brilliant focus. There are lush pages when the prose teeters on the verge of anarchy, but Jünger's passionate intensity brings everything ultimately under control. For all the feverishness of his vision, his feeling for the apocalyptic, he is a calm, orderly writer, methodical in the manner of the professional soldier he was.

The novel has more to do with philosophy and science than with politics. Jünger, soon to rejoin his regiment, has begun to take a different view of the validity of war as a means of solving differences from that expressed in *In Stahlgewittern*. Although the Brothers are far from pacifist they come down in favour of spiritual resistance, and the whole atmosphere of *Marmorklippen* is one of disgust and disillusionment at interferences with personal liberty. An ascetic as much as a scholar, Jünger's fastidiousness makes him recoil from the vulgar antics of the rabble. He is on the side of order as against anarchy, but not an order unreasonably imposed.

Auf den Marmorklippen ends with the Brothers' escape to another country while their own lies devastated. What have all these sinister feuds, apart from quarrels over territory, been about, and why do they need to have been dressed up in such peculiar finery?

There is no Hitler in the novel; when the Chief Ranger is described at all it is in terms most suited to Goering, though when I first read the book in Germany he reminded me forcibly of our fat, bejewelled, bearded and jovial First Lieutenant, a master of requisition and commandeering. A sly despot who murdered twice and then, on the run, died by his own hand, I wrote about him in *Blindfold Games*.

After subsequent readings the nature of Jünger's allegory becomes more rather than less obscure, the validity of its implications more puzzling. The sensuousness of the detail afforded to plants, flowers, countryside, coupled with the brutality of human behaviour, seemed, in 1946 Germany, inappropriate and reckless to a degree. Jünger, a veteran

storm trooper hung with Iron Crosses and now safe in his
southern German estate brooding over his plants, appears
curiously detached from reality. A rock-crystal mirror and
lamp guided the Brothers to safety, and Jünger's distancing
skills bring him a similar measure of immunity.

In Stahlgewittern (The Storm of Steel) lays down the pattern of
most of Jünger's books – episodic, documentary, auto-
biographical, yet charged with a narrative intensity, a dry,
humourless lyricism. In such passages as this, written twenty
years before *Marmorklippen*, carnage is given the same apocalyptic treatment, equating death and killing agents with beauty.

> The machine-gun ammunition in the large shell-hole
> set alight by the explosion, was burning with an intense
> pink glow. It illumined the rising fumes of the shell-burst,
> in which there writhed a heap of black bodies and the
> shadowy forms of the survivors who were rushing from
> the scene in all directions. At the same time rose a
> multitudinous tumult of pain and cries for help.

In *Marmorklippen* the orgiastic savagery, with its attendant
lethal bloodhounds and writhing vipers, can seem to verge on
the ridiculous, but in *Stahlgewittern* it is for real. Jünger's
graphic descriptions of trench life and his vision of the soldier
as the sacrificial embodiment of honour, the highest calling
on his country's behalf, endeared him to both Germany's
military class and the emerging Nazis (and more recently
Neo-Nazis). His own front-line conduct was so exemplary
under fire that it was not surprising to find his books in every
German barracks and officers' mess. It is not surprising either
that many post-war Germans find him anachronistic and
irrelevant, the propounder of antiquated ideas and values
that pre-date Hitler.

In Stahlgewittern, published in 1920, years before the anti-war

novels and memoirs of Erich Maria Remarque, Blunden,
Sassoon and Graves, was written at a time when Europe was
sick of war, but its clean, unfeeling prose, the grave priestly
tone of a soldier with the sensibility, if not the vulnerability,
of a poet, turned it into a glorious memorial to the dead.
The various editions of Jünger's books reveal revisions of
attitude inconsistent with the idea of him as an undeviating
militarist. A book at first received as a tribute to the idealism of
the soldier became regarded by the end of the twenties as
documentary evidence of the horrors of war.

It was something of a relief to turn to Jünger's *Afrikanische
Spiele* (African Games), published in 1936, but dealing with
his pre-war adventures in the Foreign Legion. Suddenly bored
with school and family the adolescent Jünger makes his way to
Verdun and signs on. The book he wrote twenty years after the
event is one of his most engaging, devoid of the complexities
and arcane words that made *Marmorklippen* a struggle to read
in the original at a time when I was spending my days inter-
viewing German naval officers about depth charges and
minesweeping gear.

It begins with a typically Jünger opening paragraph, not
unlike the one that opens *Marmorklippen*:

> It is extraordinary how fantasy, like a fever whose germs are
> borne to us from afar, lays hold upon our lives, and the
> deeper it lodges itself the fiercer it burns. In the end only
> our imaginings have reality for us and our daily life is a
> dream in which we move uneasily like players uncertain of
> their parts. That is the moment when our growing unease
> brings our reason into play and sets it the task of finding
> some means of escape.

It is escape that Jünger's alter ego, Herbert Berger, is
after, more specifically to Africa. He has a lust for action "for
the whine of bullets was like the music of the spheres to me".

He imagines a desperate company of men "whose symbol was the camp fire, the element of flame".

On his journey to the recruiting office he is robbed of his watch and money but is not deterred, even by the friendly warnings he receives from everyone to whom he confides his intention to join the Foreign Legion. Berger is an innocent, not without a sense of the ridiculous, and he soon makes friends with his fellow recruits, notably Franke, a pottery worker from Dresden. They are all on the run from something or other, boring jobs or wives, or a life on the wrong side of the law. He is befriended by a nomad acrobat, with naked women tattooed on his biceps and a gift for the mouth organ.

Jünger's description of life in the Verdun barracks has an amused and lighthearted quality quite different from anything in his other books. Real characters emerge, with tricks of speech and individual physical characteristics.

In Wilhelmshaven, never having set foot in Europe since childhood, I found myself sharing Berger's excitement as the recruits are dispatched to Marseilles. Some of them desert or get into brawls, and soon Berger, officially under age, is persuaded to reconsider his decision by the fort's medical officer.

Failing to do so in time, he finds himself on a draft to Africa, which was his original intention. His fellow soldiers are permanently drunk, but Berger gets up at dawn to watch the coast at Oran rising out of the sea. Berger, like most of the newly recruited legionnaires, considers himself free to discharge himself without notice. "I was inclined to regard life in general and the various circumstances of it as a kind of journey, which you can break off at any point if you feel like so doing."

He plans to desert, having found the company uncongenial, but before he can work out a route he is marched off to a train leaving for Sidi-bel-Abbès. He is at last put through basic training routines and lectured on the care of his equipment. Considering that most of his colleagues are scoundrels, Berger is astonished to discover that garrison duties are effectively carried out, largely because of the bleak efficiency of the NCOs in charge. Poles, Germans, Dutchmen, Italians and Spaniards all mess together with only minor altercations, and whenever Berger, the youngest and weakest of them, is about to be bullied a huge man, a former sword-swallower and fire-eater from Cologne, comes to his rescue. "I could not bear the sight of his flesh – it was fat and white and looked like the leg of a boiling fowl. He was, however, like almost all strong men, good-natured and intervened to protect me on every possible occasion."

It is usually remarked of Jünger that he has little gift for character, but that is not true of *Afrikanische Spiele*. Henry de Montherlant's *La Rose de sable*, written about the same time, was another desert-based book that had found its way into the library of the Admiral der Nordse. Although a novel, written in Algiers and dealing with the colonial questions as well as with the love affair between a French officer stationed at a remote oasis and an Arab girl, it does not diminish Jünger's fictionalised memoir. Jünger and Montherlant share a certain iciness of style and heart, though in Montherlant's case the disdain is usually directed towards women while Jünger, a happily married family man, in his books rarely mentions sex of any kind.

After describing himself as being in "the landscape of a half-forgotten dream" where everything is indistinct as if it existed only in the imagination, Jünger writes, "This was clearly to be seen from the behaviour of the men who had collected here. They had all been looking for something vague – perhaps a place where the rules of life are suspended, perhaps a magic world or a lotus island. But no sooner had they seen the uselessness of their undertaking than homesickness, like a disease of the mind, laid its hold upon them. So it was truly astonishing that things held together – but after all no one obeys orders more readily than the man who does not know what he wants. The rules for maintaining order among mercenaries are very old . . ."

After a few weeks in Sidi-bel-Abbès's barracks money arrives from Berger's father to cover his release. He uses it to purchase batman-like services before escaping with a colleague to the neighbouring oasis of Tlemcen.

Resting the first night in a haystack they are discovered by a farmer and ignominiously marched off by two gendarmes, who provide them at their post with soup and wine. A pleasant few days are spent talking and drinking before an escort arrives to return them to Bel-Abbès. A ten-day spell in cells results. "Like all the other good things of this world leisure loses its charm as soon as it is thrust upon us."

When his detention ends, Berger is sent for by the Colonel and informed that his discharge has been arranged. Having thought previously only of engineering his escape, his time in the Legion and his comrades suddenly seem dear to him. Provided with a railway pass to Oran, he begins his journey home via Marseilles and Nancy. The sweet, dry air of the desert is exchanged for freshly fallen snow. "I felt cheerful, as if I had just been bled."

In Jünger's introduction to the 1936 edition he wrote: "There are enterprises in which it is better to fail if one wants to be cured of the eternal desire to take refuge in cherished romantic illusions. The field on which we struggle for exist-ence is staked out with geometrical precision. There can be no retreat. The exotic is one of the romantic avenues of escape." He goes on to quote a remark by Leon Bloy to the effect that the satanic and the exotic may well exist as much in the grocer next door as in any far-off place.

I had good reason to be grateful for *Afrikanische Spiele* in

Wilhelmshaven, for not only is it a sport among Jünger's
books, introducing a more relaxed, vulnerable personality,
but it revived my own longing for the sun. It had been ten
years since I left India for the last time, and during those years
I had lost all sight or memory of heat. Before coming on to
Jünger I had been reading Ernst Wiechert's account of his
detention in Buchenwald and I began to forget that there
was any other kind of life. *African Games* is a sparky, larky
book, bringing with it a whiff of Africa on the breeze. For me,
it was like a promise.

After he left the army in 1923 Jünger devoted himself to
writing studies of war, to travel and reading. He came to admit
to confusion and nervous breakdown in the wake of his experiences and with the coming to power of the Nazis entered on
a period of virtual retreat, occupying himself in a similar
fashion to the Brothers in *Marmorklippen*. He did, however,
publish *Der Arbeiter*, his views on what he called the relation-
ship between armament and culture a year earlier. *The Worker*
is a detailed analysis of the evolution of societies towards total
mobilisation and the development of the individual to a point
where he loses all individuality and becomes simply an expert
mechanic, like Spengler's technician, whose sole value lies in
his ability to perform flawlessly a necessary function in the
machinery of the planned State. This thesis Jünger proposes
with some detachment but also as a prediction. His distaste
for what was going on around him led him to write later:
"I am seized with loathing for the uniforms, epaulettes,
medals and weapons whose splendour I have so loved." But he
took no active part in any kind of political protest.

After evenings of bridge-playing and drinking in the
wardrooms of Wilhelmshaven and Buxtehude, the smell of
salt coming through the windows of the one and that of pine
woods from the other, I came to Jünger as to a learned friend.
The Germans I discussed him with spoke with a kind of

reverence but also a shrugging of the shoulders, as if he was someone to be wary of. Jünger, to the conventional army or naval officer, must always have represented an intellectual challenge. In their profession such men are not encouraged to question ideologies, simply to execute policies. Jünger at one time came close to arrest for his interest in the plot to kill Hitler, the fate of the Prince Sunmyra in *Marmorklippen* paralleling that of Count von Stauffenberg after the failed assassination. Later, after the German surrender, he was for a while regarded with suspicion by interrogating Allied officers. So famous and erudite a student of warfare, with his military record and more recent role as an officer in the occupying army of Paris, was bound to excite interest. Quite rightly, he was left in peace with his books and plants.

I was, then, less interested in the morality of Jünger's behaviour than in his curiously German application of science and aesthetics. With their echoes of Goethe and Novalis, their characters' single-minded ability to separate reasearch from ethics, his books encapsulated the blinkered idealism that had brought Germany to its present state. At Oxford I had read my share of Kant and Hegel, Nietzsche and Schopenhauer, without taking in the relevance of much of their philosophy. In the Germany of 1945 one began to feel that the less thinking in the abstract that was done the better, that the facing of practical problems in a humane and tolerant way, unencumbered with grand visions of philosophical programmes, was more useful.

Jünger's detachment and clarity of observation made reading him, despite an imperfect knowledge of the language, an instructive business, like working out complicated bridge problems. The diary form, in which much of his writing is done, provides a sense of immediacy that makes one live his experiences with him, and during the winter of

1945–6 I was only too grateful for intellectual companion-
ship, no matter how bizarre the context.

Hamburg. Despite Rose Macaulay's advice that one should
always visit and consider countries at their extremes of climate
I always associate Hamburg with mellow autumn. There
were freezing days after Christmas, and terrible winters in
the rest of the decade, but in those months when I had the
occasional loan of Admiral Doenitz's Mercedes and former
chauffeur – by courtesy of appropriation by our own Flag
Officer – I see Hamburg carpeted in leaves, flurries of brown
taffeta swirling along the grassy slopes of Harveste Hude and
into the sail-spotted waters of the Aussen-Alster. We would
drive in after the day's work in our Buxtehude barracks,
Richter dropping me off at the Atlantic Hotel, before carrying
on to see his family at what was left of their block of flats in
Altona. At the Atlantic there were naval officers from our
bases at Kiel, Lübeck and Cuxhaven, former colleagues from
the 16th Destroyer Flotilla and the MTB base at Felixstowe.
There was no shortage of drink or food, and what guilt there
could have been at the contrast between our situation and
that of the local population soon evaporated after a few
Horse's Necks, our standard drink at the time.

Sometimes Richter would leave me at the quarters of an
attractive Wren Officer, with whom I had done my training
in German signals and code some years earlier, and on other
nights I visited German friends like Ernst Rowohlt, the
legendary German publisher, with whose son Ledig I later
became friendly. Jünger had exchanged his Berlin publisher
Mittler, who had brought out *In Stahlgewittern* and his next two
books, for the Hamburg firm of Hanseatische Verlagsanstalt.
From 1926 to 1939 they had been responsible for all his
books, including *Auf den Marmorklippen,* but for *Gärten und
Strassen* he had reverted to Mittler. I had no idea where Jünger

was at the time but I hoped some contact could be made through Hanseatische Verlag. Their premises turned out to be non-existent, victims of the endless and devastating bombing raids that Hamburg had to endure.

Converted to Protestantism in the sixteenth century and safely insulated from the divergent features of the rest of Germany by its membership of the Hanseatic and Customs League, Hamburg had become the most important port in Europe by the outbreak of the 1914 war. At the end of that war Germany was deprived of its merchant fleet, a loss more serious to Hamburg than the navy we were in the process of dismantling.

On those days when the Mercedes was not available – it was shared out between officers on request – I would be accompanied by a Marine driver on what he called his "wagon", a species of Jeep. I had business in the port quarter of St Pauli, from where we would take a launch across the Elbe to the Blohm and Voss shipyard, with its huge dry dock. Night after night during the war these docks would figure on the news as targets for our bombers.

You could still in those days smell the spices and tobacco stored over the centuries in the warehouses lining the canals of the Speicherstadt, though what used to be hoards of coffee in these robust neo-Gothic establishments had long since disappeared.

In better weather we would cruise in our wagon along the banks of the Aussen-Alster, along the curve of Glockengiesser Wall, Lombardsbrücke and Gorch-Fock-Wall, and pick up a boat in Hafenstrasse. From here you could sail upriver, the copper domes and spires of St Michael's and other harbour buildings breasting the railway and shipping offices, and smell the malt drifting down from the fortress-like Bavaria brewery. You soon come to Blankenese, an old fishing village that has become the haunt of Hamburg's bohemian rich.

On a steep, wooded hill the creamy baroque villas look over the river and towards the Altes Land, that once marshy area, now farmland, with its steeply-roofed, thatched barns and orchards, through which I could sometimes ride with my friends in the Staffordshire Yeomanry, the ostensible guardians of our barracks. In Blankenese's flowery, terraced restaurants and bars, its narrow winding streets, at whose every turn you could see tugs, trawlers, tankers, liners, yachts, one could feel hints of the lost café life one had read about and which would soon re-emerge in Montparnasse and the South of France.

The Marine drivers were less impressed with the sophisticated semi-rural surroundings of Blankenese, preferring to double back to St Pauli and test the cruder delights of Herbert Strasse, where half-naked women in seductively lit rooms open to the street tapped on their windows with fans or cigarette holders. Herbert Strasse was technically out of bounds to all ranks, but some of the women, in black silk stockings, high heels and little else, offered pleasures beyond our reach in Buxtehude. We would return to barracks with Ilse Werner and Zarah Leander singing on the wagon radio and the driver looking like a cat with cream on its whiskers.

Hamburg, which hosts three symphony orchestras, is also the city of Brahms, Handel and Mendelssohn-Bartholdy among composers, of Lessing and Heine among dramatists and poets, but though one or two of us occasionally visited the opera, lack of easy transport and the hour's drive in each direction kept us in barracks most evenings. The Reeperbahn's cabarets had yet to get going and the non-fraternization policy instigated by Monty was strictly adhered to, officially anyway.

Once the initial fear of reprisals had worn off, I would take any tram going, to the Stadtpark in Winterhude, or Planten un Blomen, and wander about with a book in my pocket. In

Hagenbeck's Tierpark, I had my photograph taken by the zoo's beautiful animal photographer, declining the company of a boa constrictor. When there was less time I would concentrate on the network of small canals, the Fleet, off Neuer Wall and Admiralitäts Strasse, with their arcades and empty shops, their churches and magnificent civic buildings in ruins. I became a connoisseur of rubble, a fantasist about what had been and what would be, guided only by etchings and old maps.

The canals became magnets for suicides, swollen bodies floating like hammocks in the green swill, and in the shops off Jungfernstieg artificial limbs outnumbered all other offerings. My friend Bill Purkiss, with whom I had opened the bowling at Haileybury and who followed me into the Oxford XI, lost both his legs in the last days of the war on the outskirts of Hamburg. A lieutenant in the Northumberland Fusiliers, he had been slightly wounded and was on his way to a military hospital when the lorry in which he was travelling, his legs dangling over the back, ran over a mine. Every shop I passed with its grisly furniture was a horrible reminder of him lying in his hospital ward learning to walk.

"*Mein Schatz muss ein Matrose sein,*" they began to sing again in the sailors' haunts off Seilerstrasse and Friedrichstrasse, in the Café Keese and Café Lausen, with their lavish orchestras, in the Reeperbahn. There were always sailors off the Elbe ships on the prowl, half drunk, wanting to make the best of whatever there was. In St Pauli, with its night-time glitter of light on water, shipyards, warehouses and clawing cranes on the quays of Steinwerder, the bars and billiards halls, of Brecht and Weill came to life. This was the fulfilling dream at the end of voyages, accordion music and smoke and girls twining themselves round the legs of matelots newly arrived from the tropics or Iceland, from Havana or Yokohama.

It was not always sweetness and light in the area, after

immediate post-war docility. There were squabbles among refugees from the east, and in due course clashes between the homeless and the police, demonstrations and manifestos and marches. It soon calmed down, the rubble was cleared away, temporary accommodation was arranged. The port began to hum, like the generators of a ship beginning to get steam up.

There came the day when I had to leave, to say goodbye to Richter and the Mercedes, to the Marines and the "wagon", to the country gentlemen of the Staffordshire Yeomanry, to the Atlantic Bar and the submarine captains become friends. For most the war was winding down, they would be home and unemployed in a few weeks. Uniforms would be put away in a cupboard or left to rot in an attic. Demob suits, not bell-bottoms or battledress, would be the order of the day. The German navy had been cruelly cut down to size, it would be our turn next. For me, however, there was another stint to do, a few more months to put in on the banks of the Weser. Jünger and my German dictionary still had some life in them.

Hamburg–Wilhelmshaven

HAMBURG 1997. WE check into an unremarkable hotel in Adenauerallee, a few minutes' walk from the Hauptbahnhof. Can it really be half a century since I was first here, wandering among the wreckage, interrogating German naval officers, showing off a little? I have been here several times since, observing Hamburg's youth and adolescence, its convalescence as a modern city. Now, save for a few pockets, it has come to full bloom. A city of canals more numerous than in Venice, of domes and spires sea-green over white buildings like liners, of parks running down to still, swanned and yachted water, of a great working river, its machinery writing out its uses against the sky, and especially of shipping, of rope-smell and tar and oil and salt blowing in off the North Sea. This was a seafaring place, of solid, prosperous businessmen and burghers, bankers and ship-owners, never a Nazi city, except at the last by duress. There was no confrontation, as in *Marmorklippen*, with the forces of evil, merely a professional indifference, the shrug of a society built to last on solid foundations. The Nazis came here as they had to, and were received, but without enthusiasm.

The weather this week is not mellow autumn but freezing January, the coldest recorded for decades. The streets are snow-spotted, traffic slushing over rags of ice, the canals frozen. The Alsters are looking like Lowrys, dark-clothed clusters of people skating, sliding, standing, over-excited dogs barking with pleasure.

We are here on a pilgrimage to Wilhelmshaven, but before that a day on the Elbe. First stop, the pavilion-like Kunsthalle,

off Glockengiesser Wall, with its wonderful Caspar David
Friedrichs – the *Eismeer* of 1823, its slabs of ice-like collapsed
buildings, and *Meeresufer in Mondschein,* a painting of melancholy beauty with distant sailing ships like quill pens on
moonlit water. Not only sea pictures though, but small rural
scenes with the clarity of Max Ernst. In other rooms Dix,
Nolde, Feininger, Kandinsky, Munch, Kirchner, Macke, all
fastidiously chosen, a lovely, pearl-grey Corot, Christian
Morgenstein's 1855 dunes. Some Oskar Schlemmers, too, a
relative of my old friend from TS19, who seems to have died
in 1943, a bare two years before TS19's final voyage. I suppose
all these must have been there in 1945, or in storage, but
I can't remember ever inquiring. The drivers of wagons had
other fish to fry and the general impression was that almost
all German art of any consequence had been looted.

We lunch off fish soup at an old favourite in St Pauli, the
Uberseebrücke, a glassed-in bridge almost on top of the river
and overlooking the *Rickmer Rickmers,* a century-old wind-
jammer. Jostling for space along the river front is an armada
of customs boats, tugs, trawlers, ferries and freighters. The
tiny, red Hamburg tugs, with their black funnels and dogged
persistence, as they haul ships fifty times their size to their
berths, are an abiding memory of earlier days, reproduced in
several famous paintings.

The Elbe this week, except for a narrow channel in the
middle, looks like an enormous pane of glass that has cracked.
Snow drips from the frieze of cranes on the Blohm and Voss
shore and the few boats not stranded at their moorings
have to push through loose ice. Gulls and gannets perch on
floating rafts of ice like tobogganers. I have never seen the
Elbe like this, a free-for-all for smugglers with the Customs
fleet ice-locked and deserted.

The predominating smells are of fish and malt, the
Fishmarket sluiced and silvery under the baroque gaze of

St Michael's church and the baleful glare of the fortress-like, blood-red walls of the Bavaria brewery. There is a restaurant with spectacular views at the top and we dined there later. Hamburg is famous for thick soups, as well as Hamburgers, most of them with a potato base and chunks of meat, fish, crab, shrimps thrown in, a meal in itself. Pears, beans and bacon, a delicious eel soup, and, in the *Austernstuben*, oysters, often eaten with cheese and red wine, are other specialities.

A refinement from the old days in Bernhard-Nocht Strasse, one street up from the river, is the establishment of a Museum of Erotic Art, a formalising of the area's main interests. A man called Claus Becker acquired in 1990 a remarkable collection of erotic objects and paintings. He bought up a group of rickety wooden buildings, ready for demolition, restored them and installed his collection. These are now laid out, labelled, and generally presented with a fastidiousness not out of place in the Louvre.

It was the novelist Witold Gombrowicz who, just after the war, raised the idea of a Ministry of Erotic Affairs and in the handsome catalogue to the permanent exhibition a number of respectable names like Walter Benjamin put in their six pfennigs' worth of approval. All the expected artists are there – Grosz, Dix, Fuseli, Corinth, Hogarth, Daumier, Pascin, Delvaux, Forain – with Chinese and Japanese painters excelling. Almost every species of pleasure is catered for, but when laid out so antiseptically and respectably pornographic art soon palls. The protagonists become no more sexually arousing than gymnasts at work, the furtiveness of lust neutered by authorisation, guilt by approval. In the cabarets of Grosse Freiheit, off the Reeperbahn, real men and women perform the rituals of lovemaking with varying degrees of enthusiasm, sweat and skill. The result may not exactly be art, nor the choreography memorable, but the atmosphere is more congenial and involving than in the museum. The performers mingle in the bar, dancers sit on the laps of sailors, there are schnapps and beer, music by Kurt Weill and others. It's not the pre-war Berlin of Sally Bowles and Isherwood, Spoliansky and Hollander, Dietrich's song-writers, but Hamburg's feeling of sexual adventure is what a seaport ought to have. On my last week here in 1946 I spent the evening in the Salammbo club with a grizzled Scottish engineer due for demobilisation. We drank a lot, he went upstairs with a fiery Polish stripper, and we eventually returned to barracks in Admiral Doenitz's Mercedes and the safe hands of Richter. By ill chance my friend mistook the floor of his cabin and fell asleep in the bunk of a snoring stoker. The stoker complained and the engineer was court-martialled. No impropriety was alleged, nor could there have been after a night with the Pole, as was unsuccessfully claimed in defence. He had served twenty-five years without a blemish.

Although the troubles of the deckhand narrator of B. Traven's *The Death Ship,* who finds the *Tuscaloosa,* an American freighter, has sailed without him, begin in Antwerp, the book always reminds me of Hamburg, because that is where I first read it. His ship's departure has not only left the sailor stranded without money, it has also removed his identity. A sailor without paybook and papers does not exist, except as a nuisance, forever destined to scrounge and wheedle.

Little of Traven's novel takes place at sea, since the sailor finds great difficulty in getting any captain to take him on. He gets passed from office to office, consul to consul, before a slice of luck takes him to Paris. When asked by the consul there if he has the means to stay long enough for his citizenship to be established, he exclaims, "How could I, Sir? I am a sailor. I have to look for a ship. There are no ships in Paris. I am a high-sea sailor, not a sailor of vegetable boats on the River Seine."

He is shunted out to Holland, hitch-hikes in and out of

Rotterdam, is put inside for vagrancy. Back in Paris he joins the Paris–Toulouse Express without a ticket. He has a name, Gerard Gales, but pretends he is a German, is apprehended and put in cells at Toulouse. On his release he wanders about aiming for Spain, but short of the border finds himself in the grounds of an ancient castle which turns out to be a French fortification. He is arrested, threatened with execution, and given a good meal.

On his way again he shuttles between Seville and Cadiz, sleeping rough, generally hungry. His stoical good nature and sense of the absurd save him from despair. Offered food and lodging he soon tires of it. "I should feel sick if I just had to sit around and eat. Slavery results from such treatment. You forget how to work and how to look after yourself. I should feel unhappy in a communistic state where the community takes all the risks I want to take myself. In that Spanish town I could not even go into the backyard without having someone yell after me if I were sure I had soft paper . . . If I had not escaped, there might have come a day when I would have started to kill them, one by one, for having made me utterly useless and for making me hate myself."

He stows away in Barcelona, gets lucky with a waitress in Marseilles, and back in Barcelona claps eyes on a ship the like of which he has never seen. "Looking at it, one wouldn't believe that it could ever keep above the water . . . Her shape was neither modern nor pre-Roman. She did not fit in any age I could think of." On her hull was her name: *Yorikke*. "The letters were so thin and so washed-off that I got the impression that she was ashamed to let anybody know her true name."

As the ship is about to cast off, a sailor sees him eyeing it from the jetty and calls down that there's a job going. The *Yorikke* is Liverpool-bound by way of various ports, she is short of crew, filthy and of no known nationality, like most of her sailors. He signs on. "When I was back in the quarters, which were filled with thick kerosene smoke, I knew, and this time for certain, that I was on a death ship. But I also knew for certain that it would not be my death ship, no matter what might happen to her. I shall not help the *Yorikke* make insurance."

Traven's assortment of sailors, Germans, Poles, Danes, Moroccans, overworked in fiendish conditions, make for bizarre company, each one with astonishing tales to tell. Gales becomes friendly with a German Pole called Stanislav, from Poznan, and they exchange life-stories. Stanislav, an apprentice tailor, ran away to sea but also had no papers. "This was the time when in Germany one match cost fifty-two billion marks. For this reason the Danish shipping company thought it most profitable to send her ships to the dry docks of Hamburg to be overhauled. For twenty Danish kroner five hundred German shipyard workers would work six weeks under the whip of a Socialist president who had ordered his Socialist secretary for war to break the bones of every German worker who dared strike for better wages."

Stanislav, having acquired a Danish sailor's paybook, tries all the Hamburg shipping agencies in turn, but the Germans are anti-Dane. "To hell with the Danes, who have taken our Slesvig and who now want Holstein also." What money he has saved from lifting an odd crate from a warehouse he rapidly disposes of in St Pauli.

Stanislav's story is a picaresque novel within a novel, ending up with his eventual sighting of the *Yorikke*. There is not much contact between Stanislav and Gales, both coal-drags "who live in filth, in soot, in dirt, in ashes", and the rest of the crew. "Most of the time they were cranky, cross, mad at something, sleepy whenever you saw them. In every port they got drunk, drunk as only sailors can get."

The *Yorikke* appears to have no schedule, picking up freight where it can, and avoiding the main ports of France and Italy. They linger off the North African coast, taking on board nobody quite knows what. "You see," says Stanislav, "that's why I like it on the *Yorikke*. Here nobody pushes down your throat your nationality. Because nobody has any to play. And don't you think the Russians are so much different. They are as jazzy about their Bolshevik Russia as are the hurrah nationalists of Germany. The Bolshevists shut their doors against hungry workers from the outside as close as do the American labour unions . . . I have it from a first-class Polish authority that I am not a Pole, while the Germans, on the other hand, take me only as a Polish swine. There you are."

The once repellent-seeming *Yorikke* gradually turns into a passable home. They lie off Dakar and dream of ports, of better ships. They are rarely paid.

Jn unclear circumstances both are kidnapped on the docks one dark night and shipped on to the *Empress of Madagascar*, a "funeral hussy" being readied for the seabed. They are not long at sea before there is a terrific crash and the ship begins to sink, bow first, stern high in the air. Escaping in a small boat they eventually scramble back on board the wreck of the *Empress*, now lodged on some rocks, well off any recognised sea-lanes.

Once used to their precarious position and odd angle they explore the deserted vessel, coming upon stores of drink, food, cigars. "We could lead the most beautiful life any sailor has ever dreamed of or read about," says Stanislav, "but what's all the good of it? Every day the same. That's what I can't stand. I sure do not believe there is such a thing in heaven or under heaven as what is called paradise. For I can't figure where the rich go. They can't go to the same place where the sailors go and all the communist workers."

They decide, nevertheless, on a regal banquet that lasts, with intervals, for several days. A terrific storm blows up, battering pieces from the *Empress* and dragging her off the rocks that had been clamping her together. In the end she goes quietly. "She was laid on her side and with a last gargle, ghostly against the uproar of the sea, she was buried."

A small piece of wood, part of the chart-room or the bridge, survives and they cling to it. The storm subsides and during the day they begin to feel they are close to shore. They begin to fantasize, have hallucinations, believe they can see lights of tall buildings. Then they fall asleep, tongues swollen.

On awakening Stanislav calls out, "There is the *Yorikke* . . . The death ship. She is standing by the port. Do you see the Norske ship? There she is. All glory. All in golden sun. She has iced water from the fjords. Can't you see, can't you see?"

Stanislav, more and more deranged, refuses all pleas to the effect that there are no buildings, no shore, no *Yorikke*. He lets go of his hold and splashes uncertainly into space. After a few strokes he lifts his arm and goes down, never to reappear. "He had signed on for a long voyage. For a very great voyage."

The last chapters of *The Death Ship* are among the greatest ever written about sailors and the sea, only James Hanley approaching them in their sublimity and terror, in their sense of the fragility and capacity to endure of ordinary, itinerant men, of men with neither papers, nor religion, nor fixed nationalities, but with an all-consuming need to experience, to take what comes in the process of surviving. They are short-term visionaries, humorous fatalists awash with poetry, drunk on desperation.

Every rusty old tanker on the Elbe is sister ship to the *Yorikke* and the *Empress*, every sailor in the bars of St Pauli a brother to the stateless Stanislav, dreams drowned in the deep, now as much as ever.

Hamburg–Wilhelmshaven. The main railway station in Hamburg, facing Kirchenallee, is half conservatory, half cathedral, a glass structure with enclosed glass approaches like centipedes. If any station suggests the apprehension and excitement of travel it is this one, a shining ornament among a network of canals, a radiant offering to adventure. I cannot remember if it escaped the cascade of bombs and firebombs that decimated the surroundings, but there cannot have been more obvious and fragile a target. On the radio, night after night, news used to be reported of marshalling yards in every German junction being demolished. A bomber hovering over Hamburg and seeing this glinting great greenhouse must have found the temptation irresistible.

In the old days I travelled from Wilhelmshaven or Buxtehude to Hamburg by Mercedes, sometimes by Jeep. The railways were a shambles, buses non-existent. It was a novelty, on this still freezing morning, to be taking a train.

Wilhelmshaven is due west of Hamburg, but reachable only by making a semi-circle loop that takes in Bremen and Oldenburg. The orchards of Altes Land, in spring an eider-down of blossom, are largely on the route to Cuxhaven, the North Friesian Islands and Heligoland, but we brush by the bare sticks of trees, half-timbered farmhouses and barns, before dipping south-west to Bremen, a name that always held a kind of magic for me from the great Hamburg–America transatlantic liner named after it and from Irwin Shaw's story "Sailor off the Bremen".

This is dead, flat country, the earth now looking like chocolate sponge with a dusting of icing sugar. German trains are soundless, but so potent are the images of Jews being piled into them on their journeys east that even now, fifty years later, one can shudder. Each carriage is issued with a *Fahrplan,* listing the names of stops and the expected time of arrival. It is not so much "expected" as "actual" because there is rarely a minute's difference.

At Bremen, which has doubled its capacity as a port since the war, we change trains, the original one travelling south to Osnabrück, Dortmund and Düsseldorf, sacred territory for the Rhine Army. Bremen always seemed matronly for a great port, a dignified medieval city of ancient walls, moated castles, guild houses and parks. It has a beautiful Liebfrauenkirche and old rose Renaissance Rathaus. In the picturesque port, the schooner *Deutschland* lies at anchor. The sailors' quarter of narrow streets and huddled houses has galleries dating from the seventeenth century. It is at Bremerhaven, though, thirty miles or so downriver, that you get activity of the St Pauli variety. The big ships dock here, there are as many strip-tease theatres, bars and brothels as in Hamburg, while on apparently the largest fishermen's harbour in the world, there is a museum solemnly dedicated to fishery.

We see little of all this – just a few tugs wedged in the ice under the Weser bridge – before joining a local train to Oldenburg. The distances on the *Fahrplan* are meticulously marked 12 kms to Rastede, 18 kms more to Varel, 15 to Saude, 7 finally to Wilhelmshaven. I had hoped we would stop at Sengwarden, the station for our first barracks, which lay off a country lane, with cornfields rippling like silk as far as the eye could see. At night you could hear cattle lowing, and at dawn the exercising of horses and the squawk of hens. Now it was just too far to the east.

"Wilhelmshaven", a word both romantic and sinister, used to crop up regularly on our radio interceptions from U-boats and their escorts. It was their home port and became as familiar to us as to them. Wilhelm II of Prussia set it up as a naval base in 1854, and in German ears it has a magical ring. E-boats sailed from here for attacks on our convoys year after year. The coast around is as flat as a pancake, the Ems–Jade canal cutting across the back of the port and turning it into a miniature island. Apart from its naval significance, its easy access to the East Friesian Islands and Heligoland, Wilhelmshaven's reputation for most of its life has rested on its mud baths. I don't think these were sampled by any of the Flag Officer's staff, nor were we long enough there in summer to enjoy the miles of empty, reed-fringed dunes that join the Weser estuary to the North Sea.

I remember the town as mildly unprepossessing, a spread of drab houses off twin causeways joining the port to the railway station. German sailors, waiting for interrogation and discharge, kicked their heels in converted barracks, their officers, mainly off destroyers and E-boats, doing their best to seem at ease. Hitler had put it about that captured crews would suffer terrible retribution at our hands and it took some time to recognise that fear, mixed with a certain cockiness, was responsible for their demeanour.

Now, getting off the train, we were in for a surprise, the old station in the process of demolition and a fortress-like block, in a newly made piazza, ready to take its place. New buildings were going up everywhere and it was plain that Wilhelmshaven, reduced navy or no navy, was flourishing. Oil had come to its rescue, tankers and container ships unsightly additions to the coastal fleet plying between the seven Friesian Islands. The Weser estuary runs deep into Jade Bay and soon, no doubt, this ancient countryside, with its moated castles, cows and blustery air will be unrecognisable.

There was another surprise, for when our taxi deposited us at the Columbus restaurant that overlooks the Heligoland ferry port there was no sea to be seen. Instead, there was ice reaching to the horizon, a rough carpeting of snow on it, but the sea itself invisible. I do not remember, at the depth of winter, the seas off Murmansk and Archangel, the White Sea even, icing up like this. This was the sea of Caspar David Friedrich's *Eismeer*, seen in Hamburg only days previously, or the *Winter Sea* of Paul Nash, his *Totes Meer* even. There was no liquid, just chunks of ice piling up like paving stones, dirty grey, blue-veined, violet-sheened, an X-ray plate marked with nerve-racking scratches.

As we watched over lunch, there began faint signs of movement, small channels opening near the shore and slivers of ice racing past until they beached themselves at the foot of the sea wall. There were creaking sounds, as if some undersea beast was trying to heave itself free, a conspiratorial hissing, snake-like, or like escaping gas.

In the ferry port small freighters and trawlers were stuck fast, and up river the scarlet fire-ship *Weser* and a clutch of corvettes clung to their jetties, bows wearing ice like napkins. Hundreds of birds, gulls, swans, moorhens, were jammed like commuters in a patch of freed water that had been cut for them among the reeds.

This is a sailing area, and along the Weser banks dinghies, yachts and assorted craft were reduced to crystallised toys, scattered anyhow, impotent at the whims of careless children.

They are building a naval museum on the Weser, a few hundred yards from the port entrance. Its star attraction is an obsolete U-boat, U-10, beached like a porpoise on the river bank. U-10 was commissioned only in 1967, long after my day, one of the 205 class of third-generation U-boats. Its life span was thus less than thirty years and it can never have fired a torpedo in anger. Kapitän-Leutnant Orlowski, we read, was its first captain and unlikely to have seen any action. Yet the deeds of his predecessors, the captains of those legendary U-boats that roamed the Atlantic in wolf packs to devastating effect in 1942, must be sources of pride.

U-10 had its number specially designed in stylised roman on its conning tower, its three-pronged crest incorporating the black and white of the Iron Cross against the gold of the countryside, binding the boat to the sea and the elements.

The technical data, a strange thing to be struggling

through so long after it was once meat and drink, was recorded for the visitor – crew (21 men), officers (9), armament (8 torpedoes), radar, snorkel and other devices, 2 x 600 PS diesel, 2 x 405 KW generator, etc. Specialist ratings were *E-Meister, Motoren-Meister, Torpedo-Meister, Navigations-Meister,* under whom came the various mates, *Sonar, Kochs, Funk.* Presumably, in successors to U-10, more technical specialists will be required and fewer seamen of the old kind.

U-10 was now a dinosaur and the classes of U-boats I had passing acquaintance with belonged to pre-history.

The estuary mouth, with its openings and exits, spreads out like an unfinished jigsaw. In summer these tiny harbours with their enfolding jetties are slivers of blue, avenues of trees at their backs and on the western fringe the dumpling-like oil containers. Soon what was naval will be swallowed up by the octopus spread of commerce. For now there were still ghosts of glory, if only in the minds of those who berthed here, who set out in their marauding flotillas or came limping home for sanctuary and sustenance. For the moment there was no blue, no green, to be seen, simply ice to the horizon, creaking and sibilant, the coast in a vice.

A white sea, beyond which you could not go, the last port of call and the first. This was as far back as you could remember, beyond which there was no trespass. An endless white, existential, amatory. A whiteness on whose glaciers everything broke up, a submerged minefield in thrall to its victims. White sea of memory, of fear and adventure, of cama-raderie and consolation. White sea of the unknown, on which nothing and everything is written.

PART V

Poems 1994–6

YELLOW TRAMS OF DRESDEN

Burrowing like caterpillars through ice,
The Frauen Kirche an effigy
In an ocean of rubble,

The baroque at its far east
Memory slow to dry out.

Among ruins left to mature
Luther at his chipped bible,

The Zwinger and Albertinum
Trembling on the Elbe's lip.

At night the trams, nosing into debris,
Become glow-worms, sipping at snow.

SMOKING

Gazing riverwards he flicks a cigar butt
On to the mud, a faint brssz as it hits.

He takes in a screen of trees, the struts
And filigree of bridges, a moored barge.

A water tower, the Scots baronial Lister Hospital,
T. S. Eliot's old lodgings, shiver on his eyes.

Part of a reverie, this Chelsea seascape
Where nothing quite registers, or is over.

Absent from himself, the dull impact
Of tobacco on slime alerts him, recalls

Just such an evening off Sheringham,
Leaning over the rail, smoking.

A breeze flounces water into petticoats,
There are figures in the wake, gesticulating.

NO. 45 BUS

They have unique brakes, juddering
To a halt with the noise
Of rubbery foghorns. In the early hours,
Sleepless, they cruise Beaufort Street,
Light on the river behind them
Like marbled endpapers, swilling
Under bridges. On such nights
In convoy ships lowed like cattle,

Sixth senses warning of proximity.
Hearing them I wake sweating.
In Battersea the gold Japanese pagoda
Looms out of darkness, mist patches
On plane trees like sheep's wool
Caught up on barbed wire.

Water slips back on itself.
There's a sense of light lifting.

The 45s pass, outward and homeward,
Acknowledging each other with toots
On their horns, like sister ships
With their sirens. Drivers exchange pleasantries,
Stop for fags. On this nocturnal
Cross-river route they are like pilots
Nosing an estuary, at ease with themselves
And each other, co-conspirators.

DOG-LEG
for Polly

Front paw hung limp
As a stage curate's handshake.

That blue evening a blur
And thump of metal, mud like make-up.

Now veteran of the trenches,
Hobble-skirted, she stutters on hind legs.

And where dreams propelled her
In fruitless pursuit, ears streamlined,

Only twitches of muzzle
Convey excitements of the chase.

Lying sideways this evening, pads
The texture of throat pastilles,

Coat still shiny as oilskin,
Black as liquorice,

She shapes herself
To accommodate a chaise-longue.

And what she misses
Only occasionally surfaces

As in eyes of penitents
Pleading for forgiveness.

A CALCUTTA OFFICE

Entering my father's old office
In Bankshall Street, the cries of paan sellers
And Hooghly steamer sirens
Drifting through shuttered windows,
I feel like a thief –

The desks in the same places,
The punkahs revolving, peons on their stations,
But the whole room shrunken,
As if by his absence, an empire meanwhile
And himself come to grief.

TREE FROGS IN THE CARIBBEAN

Like temple gongs muted by ocean
They begin singly, swelling in unison,

Kling huey, syar huey,
Remorselessly repetitive.

Underbellies like the shifts of Cantonese
Clerics, they put themselves about,
Puffy politicos with palatine teeth.
Goitrous, they blow themselves hoarse.

They are indifferent to distant wars.
But in their nocturnal antagonisms
Tree frogs and cicadas, old rivals,
Provide scale,

Their choruses of squabble
Mere irritants. In these green choirstalls
Light thins from banana leaves,
Conflict reduced to hushed sibilants.

VARENGEVILLE

Chalk cliffs blue-veined as icebergs,
A flat sea carrying them.

At Varengeville the church
With Braque's doves

Imprisoned in stained glass
Clings to the cliff edge,

Clusters of sheep at such angles
On steep hillsides

They seem stuck on
With blu-tack,

Legs as uneven as golfers'
Pitching out of rough.

On fine days it is possible still
To sense the dregs

Of Canadian blood shed here,
Where waters break up

And gravestones stand sentinel
Dice-like in a spent gamble.

FOREIGN LEGIONARIES AT CALVI

Like filmstars of old, képis tipped
Forward over colourless stubble,
They suggest forts abandoned
Among sand dunes, camel trains, bugles.
Le jour de gloire est arrivé.

Their tattoos bear cliché images,
Girls' names, Marie, Chantal,
As if words might make real.
Dragons and mermaids slide over muscle.
They remind of Claude Rains and Gabin.

In camps off this fabulous bay,
Wired off like chicken runs, they drill,
Oil guns, strip engines.

Waiting for posting, they top up
Suntan, challenge in beach races.

Whatever regrets about joining,
It's always too late, their geography
Initialled by misdemeanours, history's
Accounting. We watch their lorries revving,
Mostar and Sarajevo scrawled on their sides.

CAPE GOOSEBERRIES

A sly, surreptitious taste that dries
In the mouth, dust overtaken
By a sourness turning sweet.
Their leaves are papery, scrotal.

A guest at Simonstown naval base
In the Cape, I first tasted them
The day my old shipmate
Began his sentence. Robben Island
In the distance, Table Mountain under cloud.

I remember only the fruit's acidity,
Their sweetness excised.

Through the porthole I watched
Stout Boer policemen chasing Coloureds
With a stick. They eluded them,
Slithering like eels, then diving
Among bumboats laden with fruit.

Choosing Cape gooseberries now at the store
Off Fulham Road I get a sudden

Sour stink of Africa, sweat
Drying on skins the colour of aubergine.

A sudden regret, too, for somewhere unloved
In the first place but which took hold
With its light, its cruelty, its shabby, flat veldt.

IN OPORTO

On these curved steps pouring
Like watered escalators
To the Douro, girls inject themselves,
Novices under clumsy instruction.
Needles we pick our way through
Litter doorways like spent matches.

Below us banners of wine lodges –
Sandeman, Harvey, Byass –
Turn hillsides into regattas.
On quays awash in rain
Barrels gleam humpily like snails.
Barges wear funerary black sails.

The cloying vinous stink
Around these half-developed children
Masks vomit and blood
In its freefall. Syringes
Catch the last light, wine casks
Bottling a murderous sunset.

BED-SIT, 1946

In postwar days bed-sits
And bedmates changed
With the seasons. Run out of money
For the metre I knocked

On the landlord's door
And entered. He was locked
In the arms of a woman,
Her dress on the floor.

A pink corset encased her,
Thighs mottled by the fire
Which sputtered. Legs splayed,
She was warming her bottom,

Holding a book.
I murmured apology,
She never bothered to look,
An ample, hairy woman

Lavish in the rump.
He was bespectacled and sweating,
Trying to make ends meet,
Reduced to letting.

RAIL TICKETS, PORTUGAL

Like Schwitters collages these rail tickets,
"Coimbra–Amarante 20-2-94",
Itemise sunlight off salt pans,
High-prowed boats, bedraggled skies.

Gulls scream over marshes,
Reeds stiff as porcupine quills.

At Amarante the stone bridge
Pockmarked with bullets, Paulino Cabral's
Scrawled lines of old wars
E quanto sobre a ponte, O Virgem pura
A vossa imagem se adorou patente,
Sweet days of colonies and *fado.*

Aveiro was salt stretching like snow,
Sails flapping in a south-westerly
Like washing hung out to dry.
Punched tickets, 'Campagna 189 kms',
Your name and mine. Reminders
Of history catching up on us.

DONNA SUMMER OFF LOTS ROAD

This sliver of riverside, soil soured
By gases, coaldust, sewage,
Home once of sour lives, soiled birds:
In old photos boatmen in cloth caps,
Chokers, loaf down Lots Road,
Faces kippered by smoke.
A waste land of sulphur and whippets.

Less polluted now, evening revives us,
And the river, innocent of traffic,
Salvages something, an elsewhere
Of estuaries, outlets, deliverance.
In subsidence of clamour we become aware

Of community, fraternity of dogs,
The appeasement of bridges.

Light swivels wash of police boats
As if below surface fish struggle
Against netting. Barges loll
In cross-currents, weedy mucus
Of houseboat hulls, of pontoons.
Despite everything, vestiges still of Whistler,
Greaves's dinghies upended in mud,

Oars folded like oiled gannet wings.
And outside the Cross Keys a dipping light
Lends beer mugs a stained-glass glow,
A sepulchral serenity. The tide heaves up
A straggle of boats, a loitering of drinkers
Disperse, and through swing doors
The voice of Donna Summer cuts off.

NUTMEG, GRENADA

Beside my bed a nutmeg stone,
Odourless, mouse-shaped, brown.

No sound of sea as in a shell,
Just murmur of waterfall,

Brushed scent of cinnamon, clove.
Humidity on the move.

What engages is this island's
Air of complicity,

Its craving for drama. Secret police,
Belief in UFOs, black vices.

Off tall cliffs of St Sauveur
Caribs high on nationalist fervour

Leaped to their deaths, no taste for surrender,
Pride like a virus tender

In its wanderings. Adrift on spices
The island's exhalations survive

In a bottling of ocean,
Salt-spray we wear like a lotion.

HOOGHLY ABLUTIONS

Among corpses floating downriver
A man brushes his teeth
At a ghat, spattering his dhoti.
Drops on his flesh form like sago.
With rowing motions he brushes off

Paan-coloured petals. From a pitcher
He sluices himself, two fingers
Clamping his nose. A moment of splutter
And gargle, spit made ceremonial.
Pink saris flow behind him

Like ambulatory mummies, their roundness
Of flesh inflating them. They remind
Of Degas, "women drying themselves",
The angles of haunch and elbow,
Water rubbed off skin, purifying itself.